SEBASTIAN

THE CAMBOY NETWORK
BOOK 1

LINDEN BELL

Paperback ISBN: 978-1-7390763-1-3

Cover Concept: Cate Ashwood

Content Warning: anxiety attacks, career-related burnout.

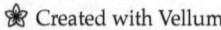 Created with Vellum

SEBASTIAN

SEBASTIAN

When your wildest fantasies come to life.

SEBASTIAN

I used to have a poster of Chris Preacher taped to my wall. And a not-safe-for-parents version hidden under the bed. But that was ten years ago, before he retired and vanished from the public eye.

Now he's standing in the middle of my new gym, the legend who inspired me to become a camboy. I have to ask him or I'll regret it forever.

Will he film one last video with me?

CHRISTIAN

I have zero complaints about my life as a run-of-the-mill personal trainer, and I have no interest in dipping my toe back into the adult entertainment business. But there's something about Sebastian's proposal that grabs me and won't let go.

Or maybe it's Sebastian himself. Sweet and sultry, nervous yet determined, Sebastian's not like anyone I've ever met— in the industry or otherwise.

I agree to just one video. But once the camera starts rolling, I don't want it to stop.

Sebastian is an age gap, nerd/jock, feel-good MM romance between an industry veteran dipping his toe back into the game and an anxiety-ridden workaholic. Expect camera-melting sex, candle-lit dinners, gentle hand caresses, and endless staring into each other's eyes. Sebastian is the first book in The Camboy Network series and can be read as a stand alone.

CONTENTS

CHAPTER
ONE

SEBASTIAN

Mars Fitness smells the same as every other gym I've ever been in. I'm not sure why I was expecting something different. A gym is a gym after all, right? But I've heard so many good things about this place that I thought maybe it would smell like a garden or a spa or something. Nope. Sweaty men still smell like sweaty men, even if they're gay.

Mars is just one of a few gyms I'm visiting and to be honest, it's pricey enough that it's not really in the running. I really only use my gym membership when the weather is crap outside and when I get the odd compulsion to lift some weights. Otherwise, I've got my daily Yoga with Adriene routine and my three-mile runs every other day, and they're more than enough to keep me camera-ready.

"Hi there, Sebastian, is it?" The big buff guy smiling at me is wearing a Mars Fitness t-shirt that looks like it's been painted onto his muscles. I can practically count the number of abs on his stomach and it takes me a minute to drag my eyes back up to his face.

"I'm Beau," he says with a southern accent that makes me think of *Gone with the Wind*. "I'm one of the owners here at Mars Fitness. Let me show you around."

I follow Beau past the front desk and into a large space packed with exercise machines. They aren't brand spanking new, but they look well-maintained.

"So, Sebastian, are you currently a member of a gym?" Beau asks.

"I just canceled it, actually," I explain. "The place is falling apart, a lot of the staff have left, and I didn't feel like I was getting my money's worth."

Beau nods like he's heard the story before. "I completely understand. We pride ourselves on providing quality equipment. Anything that breaks down usually gets fixed within a day or two and everything gets sanitized overnight."

He points to the wet wipe dispensers mounted all over the place, then takes me to the free weights area. Next to it is a small alcove with two massage tables. One of them is free but the other has a guy lying on his back. A staff member in a Mars t-shirt has the guy's leg raised and is pushing it toward his chest in a stretch.

Something about that staff member makes me look twice. He looks familiar for some reason, but I don't know anyone who works at a gym. I definitely don't know anyone who works at Mars.

The personal trainer puts the guy's leg down and walks around the table for the other leg. As he rounds the foot of the table, I catch a glimpse of his face and gasp. My heart stutters to a stop, then launches back to life in double time.

I know that guy. I know that face, those shoulders, those thighs. I had his picture taped to my bedroom wall—and a not-safe-for-parents version hidden in my underwear drawer. I used to jack off to him almost every night. He's the reason why I do what I do now.

"All our personal trainers are certified and they re-up their qualifications every year. We always end a training session with a personalized cooldown and stretch."

That's nice, Beau, but how much is just the personalized cooldown and stretch? Or better yet, how much for Chris Preacher to warm me up *and then* cool me down? Because if that's available, then sign me up!

When did he become a personal trainer? I don't know why I'm surprised. He retired from doing porn a bunch of years ago and kind of vanished off the face of the earth. I've tried looking him up every once in a while, but I've never been able to find any news about what he's doing now. I guess even retired porn stars still have to work.

Chris Preacher was the golden boy about ten years ago. He dominated the gay porn industry and was so popular that even straight porn people and non-porn people recognized his name. There were entire online message forums dedicated to obsessing over him—I might have moderated one or two back in the day. And then, all of a sudden, he disappeared. There was a short press release about retiring for personal reasons and then *poof*, he was gone.

Only to resurface at Mars fucking Fitness.

Beau leads me to the locker room, going on about cleaning schedules and how the lockers work. I'm not listening to him anymore. My mind is still back in that alcove with Chris Preacher, but now I'm second-guessing myself. Was it really him? It couldn't be. My mind has to be playing tricks on me, making me see what I want to see.

"Here are the showers, and the sauna and steam room are on the other side." Beau stops by a counter equipped with blow-dryers and hair products. There's a giant fish-bowl sitting in the corner filled with condoms and a second slightly smaller one filled with single-portion tubes of lube.

"We're all about safe sex here, so the condoms and lube are always free. Here, take one." He hands me a foil packet with the Mars logo emblazoned on it.

Right then, a moan echoes off the tile walls of the shower room. Most of the stalls are empty, but there's one with the curtain drawn closed and two sets of feet visible in the gap underneath. Just before I turn away, one of those sets kneels down and an enthusiastic "fuck" rings out.

Beau gives me an almost embarrassed look. "As long as all parties are consenting adults, we're not here to police."

I guess that's what they mean by a gay-friendly gym. I can only imagine what happens in the sauna and steam room.

Beau leaves me at the entrance of the locker room with instructions to look around on my own and then find him at the front desk if I have any questions. And I do. Just one, in fact. Is that really Chris Preacher?

I pull out my phone and quickly look up the most recent picture of him I can find. He's clean-shaven in the photo and his hair is longer. The guy in the alcove has a short sexy beard and a closely-cropped cut. But the lips are the same and the line of his neck is the same. The shoulders are about the same width, even if they look a little softer than they used to.

It's him. It's totally him. I'm positive.

I'm about to go back to the alcove to get another look, but the minute I push away from the wall I run into a solid mass of muscle.

"Oof." I would have stumbled backward but strong fingers latch around my arms to keep me upright. I look up and my lungs forget how to function.

"Hey, sorry, you all right?"

It's him. Chris fucking Preacher. He's standing right in front of me, touching my arms. I can feel the warmth of his body radiating off him. I can smell the hint of sweat from his underarms.

His brows draw together in concern and then steadily inch upward as I stare at him like I've been enthralled. He slowly lifts his hands off me and takes a step back. I almost follow him so I can stay in his personal space and breathe the air that was just in his lungs. My cock is quickly filling up and my head is a little woozy.

Oh, this is definitely, one hundred percent, without a single shred of doubt Chris Preacher. Even if I'm not sure about the face, my body's reaction to him is a dead giveaway. I don't think I've ever responded to anyone the way I do with him.

"Seriously, you gonna be okay?"

I open my mouth to say… something, I don't even know what, but the only thing that comes out is a squeak. For real. A squeak. I snap my jaw shut and nod instead. Short, jerky nods that make me look like a bobblehead, but at least the message gets across.

"Okay." He smiles like he doesn't believe me. I don't blame him. *I* don't believe me. "If you need anything, just flag down anyone wearing a t-shirt."

He gestures to the Mars logo on his chest and OMG, that chest. It's wide and thick and I can still feel how solid it was against my face. Solid with a thin layer of padding that would make it the perfect pillow to rest my head on. The shirt is tight enough that I can see his nipples through the black fabric, and suddenly my mouth is salivating for a taste of those nipples.

"Okay!" he says, a little louder. He claps his hands together and the sound jolts me out of my self-inflicted hypnosis. "You take care."

He backs away a few steps before turning and high-tailing it out of there. I slump against the wall again, banging my head lightly against it. I've just fanboyed the fuck out and made a complete fool of myself in front of my teenage idol. Good job, Sebastian.

I have to join Mars now. There's no question about it. I don't even need to visit any of the other gyms on my list. I can't pass up the opportunity to see all-time biggest celebrity crush again. I might have humiliated myself, and who knows, I'll probably squeak again the next time I see him, but at least I'll be in the same space as him. I might use the same equipment as him. Maybe even the same towel... too far?

Beau greets me when I finally make it up to the front desk. "So, any questions?"

"Nope, no, no questions. I'm sold."

"Great." Beau sets an iPad on the counter for me. "Fill this out. I'll need your credit card information. And then you'll be all set."

My hands aren't completely steady as I try to type on the iPad. That literal run-in has my body feeling all tingly and hyper-aware. I swipe my finger across the screen in a sad attempt at my signature, then hand the thing back to Beau.

"Oh, I forgot to mention that you get one free personal training session for signing up with us. Do you want to schedule that now?" Beau asks. He's looking at me expectantly as my brain rockets back to that alcove.

Chris Preacher is a personal trainer, right? That's what he was doing with the guy on the massage table, the cooldown thing that Beau mentioned. Can I request a session with him? Do I dare?

I don't know. That's like, a lot. What if I make a fool of myself again? What if he thinks I'm an idiot? Wouldn't it be better if he has no idea who I am rather than be known as that bonkers fan who won't leave him alone?

But I could be the guy lying on the massage table. I could have Chris Preacher's hands not just on my arms again, but all over me. I could be close enough to smell him again. The really foolish thing would be to walk away from an opportunity like that, right?

"Uh, yeah. Can I get a session with that guy we saw back there?" I point over my shoulder with my thumb and Beau follows my gesture.

He cocks his head to the side and narrows his eyes, then they widen with understanding. He chuckles with a knowing smile and a slow nod. "Christian? You've got a good eye. He's really popular with our members. His schedule is usually pretty full, but let me take a look and see if we can make something happen."

I wring my hands together as Beau turns to a computer

and clicks on a few things. "You free on Monday at one-thirty?"

Wait, what? Did he say Monday? That soon? Just like that? My palms tingle in anticipation. It doesn't matter if I have anything planned for that time—I can reschedule. "Yeah, I can do that."

"Cool." Beau types my name into the computer and a second later I get a text message confirmation.

> MARS FITNESS
>
> Personal training session with Christian Braga on Monday at 1:30pm. Reply with Y to confirm.

I hit that Y so hard I almost knocked the damn phone right out of my hand.

"You're all set," Beau says. "We'll see you on Monday."

I step out of Mars feeling like I've just woken up from a dream. That didn't really just happen, did it? I pull out my phone to check the confirmation text again. It's right there, nestled in a bright green bubble. In a few days, I'm going to have Chris Preacher—no, *Christian*—all to myself. Holy fucking shit.

CHAPTER
TWO

SEBASTIAN

"Can I start eating already?" Noel scowls at the rest of us while we furiously tap away on our phones.

The reality of being a camboy is that our lives exist online. If we're not stripping down for a video, we're snapping pictures of everything to keep our fans engaged on social media. It's the hustle and if you don't keep up, you'll fall behind.

Well, everyone except Noel, that is. But Noel's got that dark, edgy bad-boy reputation that fans can't get enough of. He barely has to lift an eyebrow and he'll have people begging him to fuck them. If he wasn't my best friend, I'd hate him for it. I know other guys in the industry who do.

It helps that Noel's generous with his fame. He never fails to boost our posts and make guest appearances on our feeds. I swear that half my followers are only here because of the off chance that they'll catch a picture of Noel.

The rest of us—me and Rhys and Hayden—we're at

different stages of our camboy careers, but we're all fully in the game. Which means pictures of our food and of each other and mutual tagging and posting and replying to comments from fans before we can actually get down to eating brunch.

"Sooo…" I say, dragging out the syllable until I get everyone's attention. I woke up this morning wondering if it was all a dream again. But nope, that confirmation text is still firmly in my phone and there's even a confirmation in my email inbox as backup. It's totally unreal.

I'm practically coming off the edge of my seat with excitement. They are going to lose their minds. "Remember that one gym I was going to check out? The gay one?"

"Mars Fitness?" Hayden asks. He's the one who told me about the place to begin with. A friend of a friend of his roommate went there one time and said good things about it, so he thought I might be interested. Guess I owe this Chris Preacher encounter to Hayden.

"Yep. Guess who I saw while I was there?" I get three sets of curious faces.

"Matt Bomer?" Rhys jumps in first. "Jonathan Groff? Andrew Rannells? Neil Patrick Harris? Zachary Quin—"

"No, no one like that." I wave Rhys down. Mars is upscale, but it's not Equinox-level fancy.

Noel's not even looking at me, focusing on his plate of bacon and eggs. Hayden gives me a shrug.

"Chris Preacher!"

Silence. My earth-shattering revelation is met with complete and utter silence.

"Come on, guys. Chris Preacher! Don't tell me you don't know him." I'm seriously shocked. Didn't every gay boy of my generation grow up on Chris Preacher porn? I can't be the only one.

Rhys cocks his head like he's heard the name before but can't place it. Hayden stares at me blankly—he clearly has no clue. It takes a minute for Noel to make the connection, but he eventually manages to look surprised.

"You mean that old porn guy?" Noel asks.

"He's not old," I jump to Chris Preacher's defense. "If anything, he's a legend."

Noel snorts. "Yeah, like Ian McKellen's a legend. But he's still old."

"Chris Preacher is not that old. He's in his forties." I might have looked that up to double-check. I might have spent all of last night devouring every morsel of Chris Preacher-related information I could get my grubby little hands on.

"He was at the gym?" Hayden asks, bringing us back to my point.

"Yes! He's a personal trainer there!" It's a miracle I'm not floating above my chair at this point, I can barely contain myself.

"Oh! This guy!" Rhys holds up his phone. It has a picture of Chris Preacher on the screen, probably one taken around the time of his retirement. "He's hot. He's got that daddy vibe going on."

Hayden takes the phone to study it and nods in agreement. He passes it onto Noel who hardly glances at it before giving it back to Rhys.

"Does he moonlight as a personal trainer?" Rhys asks. Of the four of us, he's the only one who's got a side gig on top of being a camboy. When he's not in front of the camera, he's on stage at a local nightclub, doing splits and spinning himself around a pole.

"No, he retired from porn a few years ago," I explain. "But he was huge back then. Won tons of awards and stuff."

"How come he's not performing?" Hayden asks. "If he looks anything like that photo, he could still attract a lot of fans."

"I don't know. He never said. At least not publicly." Trust me, I for sure would have come across it if he had.

"There was a rumor that he couldn't get it up anymore."

I glare at Noel, my hackles rising at anyone trying to smear Chris Preacher's name.

"What?" He laughs at my face. "That's just what I heard. I didn't say it was true."

Fuck. I'll never admit it out loud, but I've read that rumor a couple times too. It's not an uncommon hazard in the industry, unfortunately. Especially back in the day. Tons of performers took pills or straight-up injected 'roids into their dicks to stay hard all day. Doing that kind of stuff over a span of years can really fuck someone up. I don't see it as much these days, though. Most of us stick to more holistic approaches like regular exercise and healthy eating. There's even a paleo diet support group, I shit you not.

But Chris Preacher? No, it couldn't be that. I don't want to believe it.

"It doesn't matter why he retired," I say. "My point is, he's working at Mars now."

"Did you sign up for a membership?" Rhys asks.

"Hell yeah, I did! And I have a one-on-one session with him on Monday!"

Rhys's grin matches my own. "Whoa, that's so cool!"

"Let us know how it goes. If the place is that good, maybe I should join too," Hayden says.

Noel smirks at me. "Yeah, Sebastian. Let us know how it goes." And we all know he's not talking about the personal training session.

"I will," I say pointedly. "I was told that he's one of the best they have."

"Uh-huh." Noel's smile is still dripping with innuendo.

Whatever. Noel can joke and tease all he wants. That doesn't change the fact that I have a fucking one-on-one session with Chris fucking Preacher. I'm not going to let Noel ruin my excitement.

Beside me, Rhys's eyes light up and he nods at Noel. "No, he's right. You should see if Chris Preacher's up for a collab."

I'd be lying if I said I hadn't thought of that the second I got home from Mars yesterday. But I also dismissed the idea as soon as it popped into my head.

First of all, he's retired. And secondly, why the hell would someone as famous and legendary as Chris Preacher want to work with me? I'm not a nobody—I've done all right as a camboy in the last couple of years. But I'm not even within spitting distance of Chris Preacher's level when he retired.

It's a nice fantasy, but that's all it'll ever be. The last thing I want to do is piss him off and then get myself kicked out of the gym. "I don't know."

"It can't hurt to ask, can it?" Hayden says.

"The worst he can say is no and it's not like you'd have lost anything," Rhys adds.

Maybe… but, I don't know. Asking to have my one-on-one session with him already feels like I'm reaching. I don't want to push my luck.

"At least find out if he has erectile dysfunction. Inquiring minds want to know." Noel smirks again.

"Shut up." I scowl at Noel and this time even Rhys and Hayden glare at him.

I mean, the possibility that Chris Preacher retired because of a limp dick is not zero. I doubt he would've been able to avoid all the "performance-enhancing drugs" that were floating around back then. But I don't like the idea of Chris Preacher being anything less than the perfect specimen I remember him as.

Who knows why he retired. Maybe he met someone who didn't want him doing porn anymore—ew, no, I don't want to think of *my* Chris Preacher with anyone who isn't me. Or maybe he pissed off the wrong person and got blacklisted from the industry. There could be a million reasons that have nothing to do with his cock.

Either way, I do want to know why Chris Preacher quit. I wouldn't be a true fan if I didn't. He was at the top of his game, hugely popular and well-respected. Then one day, he hung up his jockstrap and walked away. Something had to have happened. People don't just up and leave when they've got everything going for them.

"Hello? Sebastian?" Rhys pokes me on the shoulder.

They've continued with the conversation while I was obsessing over the state of Chris Preacher's cock. Now I have no clue what they're talking about.

Noel snickers. "You're drawing up a mental storyboard for your scene with the old guy, aren't you?"

"Shut up. I am not." Though that's not a bad idea. Definitely something I wouldn't mind wasting a few hours on.

"So what were you thinking about?" Hayden asks.

"Nothing. Just, you know, zoned out."

"Uh-huh." Noel's not buying it.

Even Rhys is giving me a knowing smile. "Are you still thinking about Chris Preacher?"

"What? No, maybe. It doesn't matter what I was thinking about." I pick up my mimosa and down it, then do the same with my coffee. All three of them watch me until I don't have any more drinks to distract them with.

"Okay, fine, I was thinking about Chris Preacher."

Noel shakes his head. "Wow, you've got it bad."

I sigh. There's no point in arguing with him. I do have it bad, but you know what? That's okay. I'm a Chris Preacher fan and I don't care who knows it.

CHAPTER
THREE

CHRISTIAN

There's a name on my schedule today that I don't recognize. Weird. My client list is technically full and there shouldn't be any new names mysteriously popping up.

"Hey Beau," I call out to one of the owners of Mars Fitness and my boss. "Do you know what the deal is with the new guy on my schedule? Sebastian Silvestri?"

On the other side of the front desk, Beau glances at the sheet of paper I've turned toward him. His initial look of confusion brightens when he remembers.

"Oh, him. He's a new member. You were working with a client when I showed him around last week and then he asked for you when scheduling his intro session."

I narrow my eyes at him. "He did?" That doesn't usually happen. In fact, most of these intro sessions get assigned to the newer personal trainers who don't already have full client lists. I haven't done one of these in years.

"He did."

I lower my voice even though there's no one around us to overhear. "Does he know?"

Beau shrugs. "Beats me, but he did seem pretty distracted after we walked past you doing a cooldown."

I sigh. I guess I'll find out later this afternoon. "Okay. Thanks, Beau."

My previous career as an adult entertainer is probably the worst-kept secret around Mars. It's not something I go around announcing to anyone, but all my co-workers know and they've all been cool about it. A few of them have even admitted to seeing some of my work before. No big deal.

I don't bother hiding it from any of the gym's members either. I've had people come up and ask me about it and I'll say yes. If they ask for autographs, I'll sign whatever they hand me. If they ask for selfies, I'll politely decline. Only once has someone gotten too pushy and Beau had to step in to ask them to leave.

I'm not ashamed of what I used to do for a living. It was honest work and I was good at it. But the key word there is "used to." I'm not a performer anymore, I'm a personal trainer, and I don't want people getting the two mixed up.

Sebastian's not scheduled until the afternoon and between now and then I've got two other clients and a lunch break. I throw myself into my work as I always do, giving every client my full attention and making sure they're getting their money's worth. Lunch is a lentil salad and a peanut butter protein shake from the juice bar in Mars's lobby. Then it's time for Sebastian's session.

He looks nervous when I meet him at the front desk.

Fidgety and awkward, his hands are gripping the strap of his gym bag so tight his knuckles are white.

It's common for members to be nervous if they've never worked with a personal trainer before. I get it. It's intimidating to have this big buff guy evaluating your body and telling you what to do, especially if you're already self-conscious about how you look.

But this guy is fit. Not necessarily ripped like a lot of the guys around here, but lean and lithe with well-defined muscles and probably very little body fat. He's most likely not lifting weights, but I can tell that he's no stranger to working out and watching what he eats.

"Hi Sebastian, I'm Christian." I hold out my hand and he stares at it for a split second before he takes it.

That's when I remember. I've seen this guy before. I literally ran into him. I was coming around the corner of the locker room and he was on his phone and we landed chest to chest. He had the same stunned look on his face that he's wearing now, lips parted and eyes wide.

I'm familiar with this look. It's the one people get when they're fanboying over me. They might think it's embarrassing for them, but they have no idea how embarrassing it is for me. Once upon a time, I used to bask in that kind of attention, thinking that it meant something for random strangers to fawn all over me. But again, "used to". That was a previous life, one that I left a long time ago.

"Why don't you put your things away and I'll meet you outside the locker room?"

Sebastian nods, eyes wide, and then kind of scurries away.

He's cute.

I shake my head. What was that? Objectively speaking, yes, Sebastian's a good-looking guy with dark hair and dark eyes and lashes for days. He's got a boy-next-door quality to him. But then, almost every person who walks through Mars's front doors is good-looking. And most importantly, I don't make a habit of sleeping with my clients.

I scan Sebastian's intake form while he's in the locker room, but it doesn't tell me much. No injuries, no existing conditions to be cautious of. His fitness goal is a very unhelpful "staying fit". I keep telling Beau to take that option off the form, to no avail.

When Sebastian comes out again, he's in tight shorts and a loose tank top that actually covers very little of his torso. Oh, he works out, all right. You don't get that kind of muscle definition from sitting around doing nothing all day.

"How familiar are you with exercise equipment?" I ask as I lead him toward an alcove reserved for Mars's personal trainers.

"Uh... I know how to use them, but I'm more of a running and yoga guy." He shrugs and offers me a shy smile.

I do a double-take.

He's peering up at me through those mile-long lashes and his lips are curled into a tiny smile. It's a perfect mix of innocence and sex and it hits me low in my stomach.

The thing is, I've caught dozens of guys practicing that exact look in the locker room mirrors and I always walk past trying not to roll my eyes. On Sebastian though, it doesn't look feigned, it looks real. And it works.

I find myself wanting to smile back, wanting to let my

gaze travel leisurely down his body. That's not something I normally want to do—it's not something I should want to do at all. I rub the back of my neck and clear my throat.

"That's, uh, that's great." No more small talk with the client. Time to get down to work.

I start Sebastian out with some warm-up stretches. Too many guys jump straight into their workout, whether that's cardio or strength training, without warming up and that's just asking for an injury.

Sebastian isn't lying about being a yoga guy. He's certainly flexible enough to sink right down into the stretches I guide him through. He doesn't have any trouble with any of the other exercises I show him either. There are only a few times I have to ask to adjust his posture. He seems to hold his breath each time though, staying stiff as a board as I nudge him an inch this way and that.

At the end of our hour together, I lead him to the massage tables. "We offer assisted cooldown stretches, if you're cool with that." I go an extra step and explain what that is in case he's leery of more touching. "I basically do the stretches for you so we can get deeper into the muscle."

Sebastian stares at the table like it's a torture device.

Some clients aren't comfortable with getting so hands-on and I have no problem with that. "You don't have to if you don't want to. I can show you some other stuff."

"No!" Sebastian flushes under his olive complexion, then chuckles awkwardly. "I mean, no, I'm okay with the…" He gestures to the table and then climbs on, face down.

I smile. It's a massage table, but I'm not actually giving him a massage. "Actually, it's face up."

Sebastian flips right over. "Oh, sorry."

"No worries. It's a common mistake." I pick up one ankle to start the cool down and Sebastian's leg is as straight and solid as a telephone pole. I glance toward his face and give his leg a gentle shake. "Relax. I'm not going to hurt you."

A nervous giggle escapes Sebastian's throat and it sends shivers down my spine. Goosebumps break out over my skin and my breath catches in my lungs. Suddenly the skin under my palms feels extra warm, bordering on hot.

"So, um…"

When he trails off, I glance up toward him again. He's staring at the ceiling like he physically can't look away. His hands are clasped on his stomach and he's wringing the hell out of them.

"Yeah?" I prompt him.

"I think I recognize you." He's dropped his voice so it only travels as far as my ears.

Ah, here we go. He's seen my porn. He's most likely a fan. I take my time swinging around the foot of the table to pick up his other leg. "Oh yeah?"

Sebastian sneaks a peek at me, then goes back to staring at the ceiling. He takes a deep breath and I want to tell him to take a few more. "Are you, um, Chris Preacher?"

There was a time when that name felt more like me than my real name, when I would get confused when someone called me Christian. Now, my hackles rise just a little when I hear my old porn star name.

"Yeah, I am."

"Yeah?" He sounds relieved, which isn't the weirdest reaction I've ever gotten, but it's not a common one.

"Yeah."

His laughter is another high-pitched giggle and again, shivers run down my spine and goosebumps bloom across my skin. I take a deep breath to settle myself but the sensations don't go away.

"I thought so. I'm, um, a big fan of your work."

"Thank you," I say from behind my polite but distant mask. I've found that short and sweet answers result in short and sweet conversations.

"I actually do some performing too."

Great. Sebastian's not the first random guy to "come out" to me as a performer. They're often looking for validation, some kind of acknowledgment that we're in the same club or something. Except there are dozens of "clubs" in the industry and I'm not in any of them. Not anymore.

"In fact, you kinda inspired me to, you know, pursue this career."

I pause with his arm raised above his head. Okay, that's a new one and I don't have a canned response at the ready. In fact, I don't know how I'm supposed to feel about inspiring someone to become a porn star. Is that a good thing? What kind of kid dreams of becoming a porn star in the first place?

"Sorry, is that weird?" Sebastian looks like he's bracing for an attack and he's trying to tug his arm out of my grasp.

I gently set his arm down on the table again and step back. "No, it's, uh, flattering, I guess. Thank you." Should I be thanking him? Or should he be thanking me?

Sebastian sits up and suddenly he lights up like he's

had a revelation. He rolls his shoulders and bends from side to side. "Wow, I feel amazing."

I smile at the reaction and lean into the warm feeling it always gives me. "It's the assisted stretching. We can get deeper into the muscles this way. And you won't be as sore tomorrow either."

He jumps off the table and smiles at me, and I almost have to brace myself, it's so bright. He's been shy and nervous the entire time we've spent together and this is the first time it feels like he's dropping his guard. I have to admit, his smile is breathtaking. It's impossible not to notice.

"So, um, actually, I was wondering..." He's stammering like he's nervous, but he's still got that smile on his lips. It's so disarming that I don't hear what he says next. When I manage to tune back in, he's saying something about having a page and working together.

I blink. Wait, what? Did he—is he?

"No pressure," he says, taking a step backward like he's trying to be non-threatening. "I just thought I'd throw it out there, because like, it would totally be a dream come true to work with you. But I totally understand if you don't want to get back into the game."

He holds out a business card that he's produced from out of thin air. "Anyway, that's my page. If you wanted to check it out. I mean, you don't have to. Just, you know, if you want."

I take the card. It says Sebastian Silver, and then there's a web address below it.

"Okay, well, uh, thanks for..." he gestures vaguely around the gym, "everything." And then he disappears around the corner and into the locker room.

I stare at that corner for several long seconds, then down at the card. The answer should be simple. It should be no. So why does my heart lurch at the idea? Why do I slip the business card in my pocket instead of throwing it in the trash?

CHAPTER
FOUR

CHRISTIAN

I'm sorting through my dirty laundry when I find the card again. Sebastian Silver. I really should toss the card. I'm not getting back into the game, so there's no point in keeping it.

And yet…

I haven't been able to get Sebastian's smiles out of my head. First, that combo of sweet and sultry, then the one that was as bright as the sun. He's got that endearing yet suggestive quality that I'm sure attracts a lot of fans.

Just how many fans?

I shake my head. It doesn't matter how many followers Sebastian has. It's not going to change the fact that I'm not going back. I can't. I shouldn't.

I stare at the card for another second before putting it back on the dresser. I'll toss it later—I will.

I turn back to my dirty clothes and stuff them into a laundry bag to take to the laundromat. It's at the end of the next block, just far enough that I don't like running back and forth to my apartment between loads, so I make sure I have my earbuds with me before I head out the door.

Except, when I settle into a chair in front of the washing machine, it isn't the latest fitness podcast I pull up. I open up a search browser instead and type in "Sebastian Silver". The first result is an Instagram account. He's smiling in all his photos and I study each one like they're masterpieces hanging in a museum. They don't look contrived. He looks like he's having a good time, like he's having fun. It feels like he's inviting you into his world for a quick break, a short reprieve from reality.

I can see his appeal, the magnetism that has—holy shit —seventy thousand people following him. That's a lot of people. I don't know much about social media, but I know that seventy thousand is a freaking ton.

To say I'm impressed is an understatement and my brain immediately reframes everything I think I know about Sebastian. He's not some random guy uploading lewd selfies and calling himself a porn star. He's legit. Shit, I don't know if I could've amassed that many followers if I'd been on Instagram back in the day.

Most of his photos are solo shots with him wearing little more than briefs or in some cases, a jockstrap. Sometimes, he's with another guy who is equally naked, the two of them draped all over each other. They're the "collabs" Sebastian mentioned when he gave me his business card. The captions under the photos point to a new video release on his OnlyFans page.

There's a link in his profile and I tap on it. The second the page loads, someone sits down next to me. I jump and slam my phone against my chest so whoever it is can't see all the pictures of naked men on the screen. It's an older woman who looks like she's someone's beloved grandmother. She pulls out her knitting and when she realizes I'm staring, she offers me a sweet little smile. I nod and stand up, heart racing a little too fast, to check on my clothes and then I wander nonchalantly over to an empty corner of the laundromat. Leaning against the wall, I wait until I'm sure no one suspects anything before I open the browser again.

From the date stamps, it looks like Sebastian posts something nearly every day. I scroll through, careful not to tap on anything and inadvertently start a video. I've already had one close call, I don't trust the Bluetooth to stay connected to my earbuds and not broadcast porn to the entire laundromat.

Sebastian's prolific. Photos and videos, collabs with dozens of other guys, paid sponsorships, interviews, and industry events. I can't imagine the amount of time required to do all of that and still eat and sleep and work out.

There wasn't anything like OnlyFans or even Instagram when I was at my most popular. I worked through a studio that handled all the behind-the-scenes stuff, but even then, I had to do countless photo shoots, interviews, appearances, you name it. I was busier than I am now as a personal trainer and all I had to do then was show up on set ready to fuck. From the looks of it, Sebastian is the talent *and* the crew *and* the promotion team all rolled up into one person.

There's a wiki page on him in the search results. He's just turned thirty and has been camming since his early twenties. He was nominated for a Grabby Award last year

—Most Sex-Positive—though he didn't win. I'm disappointed on his behalf for some reason. He's publicly connected to several other well-known camboys, but I don't recognize any of their names.

A washing machine blares and I start. Damn, I've been stalking Sebastian for a good forty-five minutes and it's only felt like five. I stuff my phone into my pocket and move my wet clothes from the washer to the dryer.

I manage to stay away from thoughts of Sebastian for the rest of the afternoon only to come across his business card again when I'm putting my washed and folded clothes away.

I really need to throw the thing away. I've already satisfied my curiosity. There's no reason to look him up again. No reason to subscribe to his OnlyFans to watch his videos. I'm sure they're good. I don't need to see them firsthand.

None of that stops me from pulling out my laptop, settling onto my bed, and opening a browser. I type the URL for Sebastian's page directly into the address bar and when it loads, I hover the cursor over the subscribe button.

Don't do it. Don't do it.

I click the button and ignore the sinking feeling in my stomach as I input my credit card information.

The first video auto-plays when I scroll to it. Sebastian's sitting in an armchair, slouched down with his sweatpants around his thighs. He's got one hand on his cock and the other toying with a nipple. His smile is more sexy than innocent as he gazes directly into the camera. Directly at me.

I shift on the bed to get more comfortable. I've had a low-level hum in my groin ever since my little stalking session in the laundromat and my dick wakes up now that there's a naked cock on the screen. I palm it through my joggers and it swells against my hand.

On the screen, Sebastian is stroking himself. He's got a nice dick. Not too long, not too wide. Just big enough to catch a guy's attention and keep it. He bites his lip as he twists his palm around the head and a clear drop of pre-cum pearls at the tip. He uses his thumb to spread it around and fuck, that makes my cock leak.

There's nothing unique about that move. Everyone does it—*I've* done it. Which is how I know that Sebastian brings another level of performance to the simple swirl of finger over skin. He goes slowly, picking up drops of pre-cum on every lap. The taut skin is purple under the slick shine. He pauses every now and then to dig his thumb into his slit. His breathing gets faster and faster as he touches himself.

My eyes are glued to the screen as Sebastian runs a hand over his stomach and up to his chest. He pinches a nipple—hard—and lets out a whimper. The sound is so honest, so real, it hits me deep in my gut and my cock pulses with arousal. I want to reach through the screen and pinch his other nipple for him. I want to push his hand away and wrap my own fingers around his dick.

Sebastian kicks off his pants and hikes a knee over the arm of the chair. His hand inches down past his balls, past his taint, to a dark round shadow wedged between his ass cheeks.

"Fuck." I grip my cock hard enough to fight back the sudden urge to come. He's wearing a butt plug—Jesus Christ. In my mind, it's a big one. Or maybe a prostate massager. And he's been wearing it all day, priming himself for this video. In my mind, he's picked out the plug specifically for my personal enjoyment.

He taps the handle and gasps, jumping and tensing like he's too sensitive for that kind of stimulation. His face is scrunched up and every muscle in his body is flexed, showing off all the ridges and planes. He breathes through the pleasure and when he looks into the camera again, I'm caught.

His eyes are half-lidded, his lips are wet and parted. I can see a light sheen of sweat gathering across his brow, in the middle of his chest. His quads are quivering and his toes are curled under. He's really fucking gorgeous.

He takes the handle of the plug and twists it around. "Fuuuccck." His voice is strained, his breath hitches with each turn.

My laptop goes sliding off my stomach as I shove my joggers down low enough to pull out my dick. I'm just as hard as Sebastian is, leaking just as much pre-cum. My hips come off the bed of their own accord as my cock tries to fuck itself into my hand.

I follow Sebastian's lead. He's stroking himself with one hand and playing with the plug with the other. I reach below my balls and seek out that sensitive spot on my taint, then farther back to the wrinkled skin of my hole. I tease myself the way Sebastian does, keeping pace as he speeds up his ministrations.

He's close. So am I. His breathing is quick and shallow, audible with every gasp and sigh. He abandons the toy in his ass and palms his balls, tugging, as he concentrates his strokes around the head of his dick.

My stomach clenches in anticipation. My balls draw up

against my body. My hand works over my cock faster and tighter than it has in a long time.

Sebastian's eyes fly open when his orgasm hits him. His jaw drops in a quiet mangled cry. His gaze locks onto the camera as he empties himself in spurts all across his stomach.

It's the look on his face that sends me over the edge. The surprise, the helplessness, like he lost control of his own pleasure. I growl as cum spills out of my cock and all over my hand.

"Fuck." I haven't come that hard in ages. And certainly not from a solo video of some guy jacking himself. I roll with the aftershock of my orgasm as I watch the last of Sebastian's video through barely open eyes.

He's splayed out on the armchair, sated and satisfied. He laughs, lazy and languid. His head lolls to one side. He looks straight into the camera and whispers, "I hope you enjoyed that as much as I did."

In my mind, he tacks on my name at the end and one last shudder runs through me. "Fuck."

That was really fucking good. And if all of his videos are like this one, it's no wonder he's got seventy thousand followers. This guy knows what he's doing and he's going to go far in the industry.

Which should have absolutely nothing to do with me.

Except there's that feeling again, one that I haven't felt in quite a while. It feels like a pebble in my shoe, digging into the arch of my foot, sharp and annoying. If I walk just right, sometimes I don't feel it at all. Then there are times like this where it's positioned itself right where I'm most sensitive.

I'm not going back to porn. I can't. But sometimes, I

really fucking want to. There isn't any one thing that I miss about it. In fact, on the whole, my life is a lot better now than it was back then. Yet the lure is still there, reminding me of what I left behind, what I walked away from—of what could be if I go back.

I've been tempted in the past. People in the industry have begged me to do "just one last project" with them. I've always been able to say no. So why does it feel so much more difficult this time? Why does it feel kind of inevitable?

CHAPTER
FIVE

SEBASTIAN

It's Monday, and Mondays are admin day. I don't shoot videos or take photos or post anything on admin days. Instead, I'm updating my finances, tracking analytics, and doing all the other not-fun stuff people don't like doing.

Except I love it. I'm a data nerd. I love looking at numbers and trends and figuring out why this metric went up while another went down. I'd spend all week on admin if that was what actually generated income. But no. Apparently, fans don't pay for me to talk nerd to them—at least, not my fans.

The guys think I'm obsessive when it comes to my data. But I doubt any of them know their year-over-year growth rates or returns on investments. Listen, I'm running my own business, okay? I'm a creative entrepreneur. A camboy-preneur, if you will. And businesses that don't grow, die.

I log into my OnlyFans account and download the

subscriber data for the past week. I don't like the numbers I'm seeing. They're down from last week and last week was down from the week before. In fact, there's been a steady downward trend for almost two months now.

It doesn't always mean anything. Sometimes there's a dip in activity and that's totally normal—nothing to get worried about. Except my numbers were going up at this time last year and if I remember correctly… I pull up my spreadsheets from a few years ago. Yup, these are usually my best months.

Still. There could be dozens of ways to explain this decline. No reason to jump to the worst-case scenario. Like I'm no longer relevant, no longer entertaining. Like there's someone newer, younger, more exciting who is stealing everyone's attention.

Pressure builds on my chest, sinking into me until it feels like I have a gaping hole right under my sternum. My fingers go a little numb and I curl them into fists, then my fists start trembling, and the more I try to hold them still, the more the rest of my body starts to shake.

I can't breathe because if I breathe something bad will happen. I can't move because something bad will happen then too. My heart is vibrating more than it's beating and all I can do is sit there and stare at nothing. I might throw up.

It's an anxiety attack. I've had them before—since high school actually—and I know what I need to do. That doesn't make it any easier though, because the prescription medication I need is in the bathroom and the mere thought of getting up from the chair makes my stomach twist into knots.

Fuck. Fuck, fuck, fuck.

I'm supposed to be over this. I've done all the therapy. I've been on medication. I know all the breathing techniques and mindfulness techniques and thinking exercises that are supposed to make these anxiety attacks go away. But no matter how far I think I've come, it still sneaks up on me when I'm least expecting it.

Like when I'm updating my favorite spreadsheet.

"Fuck!" Shouting the word out loud doesn't make the anxiety any better, but it does get me breathing. I suck in a lungful of air as my heart thunders against my ribs.

I pitch forward and my laptop goes sliding off my lap, down my shins, and onto the floor. I shove it aside with my foot, then push myself to my feet. I pause for a moment because the room is spinning a little and my stomach does not appreciate the altitude change. When I don't fall over or taste bile in my throat, I inch my way to the bathroom.

Whoever decided childproof caps were a good idea for medication used during anxiety attacks has obviously never had an anxiety attack before. My fingers don't feel strong enough to grip the bottle, never mind do the press down and turn motion to open the damn thing. I'm lucky I don't spill any onto the floor—or worse, down the sink.

I swallow the pill dry and brace my hands on the counter. It's going to take at least an hour for the medication to kick in and until then, there's not much I can do except try not to freak out any more than I already am.

Okay, I can do this. I just need to get to the bed, crawl under the covers, bury myself in pillows, and wait. Simple. Easy. I do that every night.

I wrap my arms around myself and half-stumble, half-stagger to my bed. The one benefit of living in a little studio apartment is that nothing is more than a few feet away. The bed is cold when I clamber onto it. I hug a pillow to my chest and curl up around it, burying my face into the soft fabric.

I breathe. In for a count of four. Hold for four. Out for four. Hold for four. I pick out five things I can see. Four things I can feel. Three things I can hear. Two things I can smell. And one thing I can taste.

I think about something happy, something calming. The first thing that comes to mind is Chris Preacher—no, Christian. The way he gently adjusted my posture during the one-on-one training session we had. The warmth of his hands and the firmness of his touch as he worked me through the stretches at the end. The way the corners of his eyes crinkled when he smiled.

He's nice. A perfectly normal guy. Not arrogant or egotistical like famous people are supposed to be. They say to never meet your heroes, so I was marginally afraid that he'd turn out to be a jerk, that this person I've idolized for so long wouldn't be worth the pedestal I'd put him on. But I don't think that's the case with Christian. He seemed almost bashful when I asked about his previous career. He didn't seem at all interested in reliving his glory days.

Which... oh god, *why* did I ask him for a collab? *Why* did I give him a freaking business card? I shouldn't have even mentioned I was a camboy. He probably has all kinds of guys saying that to him all the time. He probably threw out the card the second I turned my back.

I moan into the pillow and the sound morphs into a yell. I *know* this is the anxiety fucking with my brain, but no matter how many times I tell myself that, the thoughts don't go away. They get louder, they drill deeper, until they're so real I have no choice but to believe them.

Christian is a freaking legend in the industry. I'm practically nobody. He's already started a new and successful chapter in his life. He's got no reason to turn around and dive back into a world he walked away from just because, what—some random dude had the audacity to proposition him?

God, what was I thinking? I'm such an idiot. There's no chance in hell he'll say yes. And if that's what I consider to be good decision-making, maybe I shouldn't be doing this whole creative entrepreneur bullshit to begin with. No wonder my subscribers are dropping like flies.

The pressure on my chest gets worse, dragging me down and crushing me. I lean into it. I let it smother me. Everything feels heavy and if I end up drowning in this, then I drown in it. I don't know what else I can do—I have no other choice.

The next time I open my eyes, it's dark. Whatever sliver of sunlight that comes through the window during the day is long gone. I must've slept for hours and I feel exhausted.

My anxiety isn't quite so oppressive anymore, so that's a plus. But I can still feel it lingering around the edges of my consciousness, ready to pounce if I let my guard down.

I'm tempted to turn over and go back to sleep, but I've already lost half the day and well, I should at least check my inbox. My laptop is still on the floor and I drag it into bed with me. There are a shit ton of new emails, just none that I want to deal with at the moment. So instead, I open up a new browser and type in my favorite search term: Chris Preacher.

All the results on the first page are purple with time stamps telling me I've already visited the site. I know that'll be the case with the second page too—and the third and the fourth. The image results, though, those won't mock my obsession with Christian.

He's just so easy to look at. Big broad shoulders. Short buzz cut I want to rub my palms over. Close-cropped beard I want to scrape across my skin. Two full sleeves of tattoos I want to trace with my fingers, then with my tongue.

He's older now than in most of the photos online and personally, I think he's gotten hotter with age. He had this stern daddy vibe when he was active and if anything, it's more intense now that he's a personal trainer. It's the air of authority he exudes. He knows what he's talking about, he knows what he's doing, and you'll regret it if you don't do what he says. It makes me gooey inside every time I look at him.

I know he's never going to take me up on that request for a collab. It was always a shooting-for-the-stars kind of thing. Like the guys said, the worst that can happen is he says no and I'll go on with my life. There will be other guys I can work with, other performers and content creators I can partner with. Even if my numbers are down for a few months, I'll find a way to bring them back up. I just have to be creative. Because this is what I do. I'm an entrepreneur, goddamn it. If one strategy doesn't work, then I'll try the next thing, and then the next until some-thing does.

I close my laptop with my little pep talk still circulating

in my mind. I'll write today off as a mental health day—
we all need those every once in a while. Then I'll get up
early tomorrow, go for a run, and put on the latest Yoga
with Adriene episode. Everything will be better in the
morning.

CHAPTER SIX

CHRISTIAN

The one-on-one session with Sebastian was almost two weeks ago, and I haven't seen any trace of him at the gym since. And not for lack of trying either. I've had my eyes peeled for that head of dark hair and that pair of dark eyes. By now, I'm pretty sure I can pick him out of a crowded room of gym bros from nothing more than the tilt of his shoulders. *That's* how much I've been watching his OnlyFans page. *That's* how much I've been distracted while at work.

"What are you doing?"

I jump at the question. It's from Donnie, the gym's resident spin instructor. He must have just finished a class because he's in his cycling gear and he's drenched with sweat.

"Nothing."

Donnie cocks an eyebrow at me. "Doesn't look like nothing. Looks like you're surveying the land. Getting that desperate, huh?"

"Shut up." I spin around and march toward the staff locker room. He knows I don't make a habit of sleeping with gym members. Some of our other co-workers aren't quite so circumspect, but Donnie and I aren't known to fuck where we eat, so to speak.

Donnie's right behind me and he starts stripping the second we round the corner into the relative privacy of the locker room. "You'll get no judgment from me. Consenting adults and all that."

It's the gym's policy—as long as everyone involved is a consenting adult, almost anything goes. Some of the stuff we've walked in on, that we've had to studiously ignore... they would fill volumes.

"It's not like that," I say, pulling my bag out of my locker.

Donnie's wearing nothing but a towel around his hips. "Hmm."

He obviously doesn't believe me and I don't blame him. My mood has been getting progressively worse with each day that Sebastian remains MIA. It's so bad now that even I'm annoyed with myself.

I have no reason to be so cranky. Members aren't required to show up at the gym if they don't want to. It's not like he's missed or canceled a scheduled session. We have no plans to meet on a certain day or a certain time. It's just... I thought I'd see him around more, that's all.

I thought he'd follow up on his proposal to work together. His business card is still burning a hole through the top of my dresser. I've gotten myself all worked up about what I'd say to him the next time I saw him. And now he's disappeared.

I'm... disappointed.

Which makes no damn sense. Porn isn't in the cards for me anymore and I should be happy that Sebastian isn't hounding me for an answer I can't give. So why don't I cancel the damn subscription to his OnlyFans? Why am I still looking for him whenever I'm at work?

"Still here?" Donnie comes back from what has to be the world's fastest shower.

I force myself to move, to switch out my Mars t-shirt for a plain one and my gym shoes for my street ones. I can see Donnie eyeing me with a concerned look, but he's not usually one to pry into other people's business.

"I'm fine," I offer because Donnie and I are friends. Because I don't want him to go mentioning anything to Beau or Gavin, Beau's husband and Mars's co-owner. Because Beau and Gavin won't hesitate to corner me and bombard me with questions. "Really, I'm good."

He nods, still unconvinced. "Okay, sure."

I zip up my bag and close the locker door. "Cool. I'll see you tomorrow, then."

"Yeah. See you."

On my way out, I wave goodbye to Sawyer, the guy who mans the front desk on evenings and weekends, then sidestep a group of people who are loitering by the little tables next to the juice bar. I push open the main doors and run headlong into someone.

Vanilla. Like a tray of gooey chocolate chip cookies. My mouth waters at the scent. It takes me a second to realize I'm sniffing someone and I take a step back to apologize. Only to find that I've walked into the person I've spent the last couple weeks looking for.

"Sebastian."

"Hi." He squeaks and glances quickly down at his shoulder.

My hands are around his arms—to hold him steady, of course, because we collided and I don't want Sebastian falling over. I immediately pull my hands back, my palms still tingling from the touch, and stuff them into my pockets.

"Sorry about that."

Sebastian's eyes are wide as he stares up at me. Up close like this, I can see specks of gold in his brown irises. They sparkle in the late evening light.

"It's okay." Sebastian's voice is quiet, just enough to bridge the gap between us. "You're, uh, on your way out?" He winces and keeps stammering. "I mean, of course you're on your way out. Sorry, stupid question."

A smile tugs at my lips and warmth blossoms in my chest. He really is cute. "It's not a stupid question. And yes, I'm all done with clients for the day."

"Cool."

I've stepped aside to let the door shut, but otherwise, my feet are perfectly content to stay glued to their spot on the sidewalk. I've spent nearly two weeks looking for these dark eyes, that dark hair, my feet aren't about to let me walk away from it now. Sebastian makes no move to open the door either. So we stand there, in front of Mars, staring at each other like that's a perfectly normal thing for two near strangers to do.

A knock on the glass door jolts me from the depths of Sebastian's eyes.

"Hey, uh… mind if I…?" It's Donnie, on the other side of the glass, smirking at me like all the dots have connected themselves and he knows exactly what's going on.

I move out of the way, drop my chin to my chest, and rub the back of my neck.

"Sorry to interrupt." Donnie's voice drips with amusement.

"Oh! No, we're not... we weren't..." Sebastian is adorable when he's nervous like this. I can see his flush under his naturally olive skin and it makes me wonder how far down his chest it extends.

"I was leaving," I say, though now that Sebastian's here, I don't want to leave anymore.

"And I was going in," Sebastian says more to me than to Donnie.

"Right..." Donnie looks back and forth between us, biting his lips like he's trying really hard not to laugh. "Well, then, I will leave you two to it."

He slips away, and thank god, because I don't know what's going on here, but there's definitely something happening between me and Sebastian.

"So, um, you're going home?" Sebastian asks, his voice taking on that soft quality again, like he's speaking for my ears only.

"Yeah."

"No big plans for the evening?"

"Nope."

He nods and his gaze darts to the door, then back to me. "I, um, was going to work out—"

"Right, yeah, I didn't mean to keep you." I go to back away from him but Sebastian follows me.

He chuckles lightly and the sound tickles like I've swallowed a sip of bubbly.

"I was going to say that I don't really feel like working out today. I mean, if you wanted to grab dinner or something?"

My brain latches on to the "or something" and takes off running. In one very specific direction. Where clothes are not required.

"Only if you don't have other plans. Or if you want to. No pressure, of course. I just thought I'd ask."

About dinner.

I push away the images of Sebastian naked on a bed, legs spread and cock hard. With how much I've been following him online, I know exactly what he'll look like all sprawled out. But he isn't asking to fuck, he's asking about dinner.

"Yeah," I say, hoping my voice is steadier than I feel.

"Yeah?" Sebastian's eyes light up almost as bright as they were at the end of our one-on-one session. "Really?"

My heart races in my chest. What am I doing? I don't normally have dinner with clients, but it is just dinner. There's nothing wrong or illicit about that. Yet it feels like a fork in the road. Turn left and go back to my life as I know it. Turn right and who knows where the hell I'll end up.

I should go left. My life is fine as it is and there's no reason to go shaking things up now. But there's something tugging me toward the right, like some invisible tether that's slowly drawing me in Sebastian's direction. "Yeah, sure."

"Oh. Um, I mean—" he points down the street, "there's a place not too far from here that's pretty good?"

I don't care where we go, it really doesn't matter so long as Sebastian's there. Despite my better judgment, I've become ensnared by his allure. It keeps bringing me back to his OnlyFans page to rewatch video after video. It has me looking for him every day at Mars.

There's something about him that's undeniably attractive and for the life of me, I can't put my finger on it. There's no shortage of attractive guys in my life. Hot guys, cute guys, tall ones, short ones—Mars is full of guys who would drop their pants for me. Sebastian's different from all of them though. It doesn't make any sense—he just is.

The bar he takes us to is only a couple blocks away.

"You have no idea how surprised I was when I realized who you were," Sebastian says after the waiter takes our drinks order. "I mean, sorry, we don't have to talk about… if you don't want to."

"What? About porn?" I would've been more shocked if this *wasn't* the first thing Sebastian brought up. "It's fine. I don't mind talking about it."

He props his chin on his hand, grinning like a kid with a giant bowl of ice cream. "Yeah? Because I think I've watched every one of your videos."

That's… impressive. I've done a lot of videos. Some dating back to before Sebastian was old enough to even know what porn is. "Really? All of them?"

"Yeah, I mean, as many as I've been able to find. Unless you have some never-before-seen footage collecting dust somewhere?"

I chuckle, because there probably is, considering how much I worked back then. "I wouldn't have access to any of that. It all belongs to the studios."

Sebastian nods. "I always forget that."

I lean my elbows on the table, bringing me closer to

Sebastian and that hint of vanilla that my nose picks out from the stale scent of beer. "Forget what?"

"Studios. That they own the material you produce."

"You've never worked with a studio before?" I think I know the answer already, but best not to let him know how much I've internet stalked him.

He shakes his head with a shy grin. "Nope. I've always been independent, running my own page. I do all the paid sponsorships and collaborations with other performers. But I get to control what I do and who I do it with. I might not make as much money this way, but at least I don't have to answer to anyone else."

"Sounds like a lot of work."

Sebastian offers me a bashful shrug. "It is. But it's all mine. I'm not at the mercy of some studio asshole who couldn't care less about me." He starts, eyes going wide, looking contrite. "I mean, there's nothing wrong with working for a studio. I know you were with studios for most of your career."

If he thinks I'm offended, he's got nothing to worry about. The big studios were indeed filled with a lot of assholes. "Only because there were no other options. Although, I don't know if I would have opted to strike out on my own, even if there was." I'm not nearly as entrepreneurial as Sebastian seems. It's why I decided to work for Mars rather than run my own client list.

"You would've had a massive OnlyFans following." Sebastian smiles sheepishly. "Actually, I think you still could if you wanted to start a page now."

I laugh because that would be an unmitigated disaster. "No one wants to watch an old guy like me."

Sebastian's gaze rakes over me, lingering on my shoulders and on my forearms. His tongue slips out to wet his bottom lip. "Trust me. Everyone would want to watch you. I'm not just saying that. My friends think so too."

"Your friends?" I ask and Sebastian's face turns an alarming shade of reddish-green.

"Um, I mean…"

He's saved by the waiter coming back with our drinks. I take a sip of my IPA, the bitter hops adding to the warmth that's been simmering in me since I ran into Sebastian.

Sebastian practically chugs his margarita.

"You were saying something about your friends?" I prompt because suddenly I want to know how much he's been talking to his friends about me.

"Right, yeah, um, I might have mentioned to a few friends that I saw you at Mars," Sebastian mutters quietly.

I have to lean in really close to hear him and in the process, I pick up another whiff of vanilla. I smother a deep moan that wants to escape from the middle of my chest. "And they think I should start an OnlyFans page?"

Sebastian peeks up at me through his lashes, all sweet and demure, and that warmth spreads down to my groin.

"They think you would do well if you had one." Sebastian's voice feels like a caress, like a gentle drag of his hand down my chest, over my stomach, and lower.

My dick starts to fill like Sebastian's just palmed it. My body shifts like it's trying to press my cock more firmly against him.

"I wouldn't have anything to put on a page like that," I say, though it comes out more like a growl.

Sebastian's eyes dilate and his lips part with a silent gasp. "If you want, I can help you with that."

CHAPTER
SEVEN

SEBASTIAN

For about two seconds, I'm absolutely certain that Christian is going to take me up on the offer. Not necessarily to help him set up an OnlyFans page or even an official collab video. But sex. We're going to have sex. I just know it.

Then something happens and Christian blinks like he's coming out of a trance. He shifts in his seat and clears his throat. He's looking everywhere but at me and I wonder if I imagined that look in his eyes. The one that said, "Your place or mine?"

I shrink back in my chair and pull my hands into my lap. I'm pretty sure I didn't imagine it. I can still feel the wisps of sexual tension lingering between us. Was it something I said? Did I come on too strong? He seemed just as into it as I was, though...

"Sorry," Christian says. "I, um, that's... very flattering. Thank you."

Flattering. That's what he said when I told him he'd

inspired my camboy career. I thought it was a compliment at the time. Now, I'm not so sure.

"I didn't mean to pressure you or anything," I say. "I know you're retired and all that."

Christian's gaze flicks to me, alert and sharp, then flicks away—so fast I don't catch the look in his eyes. He's uncomfortable, that much is obvious. There's something he doesn't want to talk about, something I'm not supposed to know.

He takes in a deep breath that expands his already broad chest. The fabric of his shirt is like a second skin, showing off every muscle as they move. Even now, having been rejected, I can't stop admiring Christian and the perfect male specimen that he is.

I need to stop. He's made it explicitly clear that he has no interest in returning to porn. Any more fantasizing I do is only going to end badly for me. I'm well-versed in finding disappointment everywhere I look, I don't need to go drumming up more just for fun.

"You weren't pressuring me."

I nod. Of course he would say that. That's the nice thing to say. Forgive me if I don't believe him. The waiter shows up again, thank god, because the fun flirty atmosphere between us has turned heavy and dense. He sets down a huge basket of fries, mozzarella sticks, and two types of wings.

"Can I get either of you a refill?" the waiter asks.

Christian looks edgy and tense when he answers. "Yeah, sure. Thanks."

I nod to the waiter too, and he leaves with our empty glasses.

Christian clears his throat again and shakes his head

once like he's trying to clear something from his mind. "Sorry about that," he says. He flashes me a smile, but it's still too strained to be genuine.

"Is…" I'm not sure I should ask. Is it prying? Am I crossing a line? "… everything okay?"

Christian takes another one of those deep breaths and I try not to let my gaze drift to his chest, I really do. It's hard, though. There's so much of it, and it's so enticing as it moves.

"Yeah, just…" Christian glances up at me and our gazes collide.

My lungs seize at the depth of emotion in Christian's eyes. There's a lot going on in there and I have no idea what any of it means, but I have a distinct feeling that we've stumbled on some old wound that might not be completely healed.

Christian tears his gaze away and I want to chase after it. I want to drag him back and figure out what happened, what hurt him, and what can I do to make it better.

I can't do any of that though. It's not my place. I might know every detail about Christian there is to know on the internet, but for all intents and purposes, we're still little more than strangers. One personal training session and half of a dinner doesn't make us anything more than acquaintances.

"So, can you tell me more about your business?" Christian's voice is rough when he speaks. "How long have you been camming?"

I reach for a fry and finish eating it before I answer. The air around us is thick with whatever is going on in Christian's head, with all of my unasked questions. "Since college. I drew up a business plan for a class project."

Christian's hand hovers in midair, holding a mozzarella stick. His eyebrows shoot up to his hairline. "You what?"

I smile at his stunned reaction and some of the weight in the air dissipates. "I was a business major in college and I had to develop a complete business plan for one of my courses. Like, start-up costs, operating budget, product development, marketing plan, the whole works."

"And you did a camboy business?" Christian's expression is equal parts fascination and horror and it makes me smile wider.

"Yeah," I say with a laugh. Sometimes people don't believe me when I tell them this story. They think I'm making it up to show off or something, though I'm not sure how being a verified nerd is anything to brag about.

"And your instructor was okay with that?"

I shrug. "Actually, she thought it was a great idea. No one else had ever tried anything like it before. She said it was very appropriate for today's economy."

"Today's economy?"

"Yeah, you know, influencers, content creators. She liked that I was applying traditional business concepts to something new."

There's a furrow between Christian's brows as he looks at me, really looks at me, like he's studying me, like I'm some new creature he's seeing for the first time.

It makes me squirm in my seat. It makes me want to hide in delighted embarrassment. It makes my simmering lust for him bubble up to a boil.

"That's... incredible," Christian says.

I bite my lip because, OMG, the way he says that, quiet and dripping with awe, it makes my heart go all pitter-patter. Chris Preacher thinks I'm incredible. Me. Little, insignificant, anxiety-ridden me. How the hell is that even real?

He's the incredible one. The crush I've harbored for years, the infatuation over this smoking hot celebrity, it builds inside me. Christian is way hotter than Chris Preacher. He's got the personality that goes with the looks—he's genuine and kind in addition to being gorgeous. Now that I know this version of him, that crush is quickly growing into something more, something dangerous.

His gaze heats me up and the longer he stares at me the hotter I get. I wasn't imagining it before, there was some crazy chemistry brewing between us and it's starting to react again.

Christian feels it too, I'm sure of it. I can see it in his eyes, the way they darken, in his lips, the way he licks them. He looks like a predator out on a hunt, and yeah, I'm the prey.

"I don't do porn anymore," he says, answering a question I didn't ask. "I have my reasons."

There's all that emotion again. It's in his voice this time, it's rolling off him and hitting me right in the chest, making it hard to breathe. I don't say anything because I hear a silent "but" in there somewhere.

"I like my life as it is." It almost sounds like he's talking to himself, like he's trying to convince himself.

My chest constricts and I want to give him a hug. I want to hold him and comfort him until whatever this is passes. Then I want to know what it is that could possibly have hurt him so much. It's not my place to do any of this, but that doesn't make me want it any less.

"You've built a good life for yourself," I say quietly, trying to console the melancholy out of him.

His lips curl up, but it doesn't look like a smile. "It *is* a good life."

When he doesn't continue, I whisper, "But?"

He rubs the back of his neck and lets out a haggard chuckle. "But. There shouldn't be a 'but,' and yet, there it is."

"Do you want to talk about it?" I hold my breath.

Christian doesn't answer for several slow breaths, then takes a long drink of his beer. "But…" He shakes his head. "Why don't you tell me what exactly a 'collab' would involve?"

I gasp as the vise around my lungs suddenly loosens. My pulse skyrockets and blood *whooshes* past my ears. OMG, this is really happening. Christian is considering a collab with me. Holy fucking shit.

"Uh, well, it really depends on us and how we want to structure it." I don't sound like myself. Or rather, I don't sound the way I feel. Inside, I'm in nuclear meltdown mode, alarms clanging and my mind spinning trying to figure out what it needs to do next. But words are flowing out of my mouth like I actually know what I'm talking about.

"With the guys I've worked with in the past, we shoot enough footage so we all have enough material for our respective pages. But since you don't have a page, I can host the video on mine and we can split the proceeds. I'll make sure to provide all the reports, you know, for full transparency."

Christian actually grins at that last part. "I have a

feeling I don't need to worry about you short-changing me."

I smile back at him and shrug. "You never know. Just in case."

"And what about production costs?"

The question sends a disproportionate thrill through me—does he want to talk profit margin? Does he want to see my spreadsheets? I clasp my hands in my lap so I don't start waving them around in excitement.

"Production costs are pretty low. I already have all the equipment, so we'd only need to find a place to film. We can do it at my place since it's all set up already."

Christian nods like that all makes sense to him.

"I have a standard contract that lays it all out, if you want to take a look at it. It's all open to negotiation, of course."

Christian's eyes crinkle at the edges as he smiles and my heart does a somersault in my chest. "A standard contract, huh? Sounds legit."

"Yeah, well, I try." My heart somersaults again.

He growls—it's probably just a hum, but it sounds like it's coming from deep in his chest. It reverberates through me and I shudder in response.

Under the table, I pinch the skin on my wrist. The restaurant doesn't vanish around me, so this must be real. I'm not dreaming or hallucinating. I'm actually talking to Christian about working together. He actually looks like he might say yes.

"You've given me a lot to think about," he says.

Oh god, say yes, please say yes. "Do you, uh, have any other questions? I can send you everything to review.

There's the contract, but I have other stuff too, like a content usage guide, sample marketing plans, hard and soft limits list—" I snap my mouth shut to stop myself because I'm rambling and Christian's giving me that grin again.

"You've thought of everything, haven't you?"

"I'm sure there's something I've missed." Like a guide on what to do when you're chatting with your biggest celebrity crush about shooting a porn video together.

Christian nods. "Send me what you've got."

I swallow down the sudden wave of happiness that threatens to overwhelm me. It rises up, filling every nook and cranny, until it feels like I'm going to burst with it. I want to jump up and down. I want to call the guys and tell them everything. I want to sit and cry because I really can't believe this is happening to me.

I nod and swallow again so I can actually speak. "Yeah, no problem. I'll do it when I get home."

Christian takes that deep breath and his chest expands. He lets it out slowly and when he speaks, he sounds a little shaky too. "Awesome, I'm looking forward to it."

CHAPTER
EIGHT

CHRISTIAN

I click on Sebastian's email and stare at the number of attachments listed at the bottom. I'd be annoyed if I wasn't so amused. When Sebastian warned me that he liked having everything documented in writing, I hadn't realized he meant a literal mountain of paperwork.

Some of it is standard stuff I've come across in my studio days: a general consent form, a basic talent information form, and an STI testing form. The contract is impressively long, with sections I've literally never heard of and, to be honest, don't quite understand. Then there's the hard and soft limits form, a content usage guide, and the marketing plan that Sebastian mentioned during dinner. He even sent over his most recent STI screening results, dated last week, and a signed statement that he's on PrEP. I don't remember seeing half this stuff back then.

Do I really want to do this?

It's not the paperwork—scribbling my signature on the dotted line is the easy part. It's everything that comes after.

Putting myself on display, living up to public expectations, chasing the high of external validation...

I push my laptop away and wander into the kitchen for a beer.

Am I getting too caught up in the allure of Sebastian to think clearly? Sitting across the table from him, listening to him talk about his work, it was so easy to get swept up in the excitement of it all. The rush from releasing a new video, and the exhilaration when fans love it. Being wanted, adored, admired. It's a heady feeling that defined so much of my life.

My porn star years were everything you would've expected them to be. Big paychecks. Expensive clothes. Luxurious gifts from random strangers. I got flown all around the world in first class. Posed for photo shoots in the most beautiful locations. Fucked super hot guys. Indulged in all the drugs and alcohol my body could handle.

It had been great until it wasn't. Until I couldn't remember what city I was in when I woke up in the morning. Until entire days and weeks went by in a blur because I was getting pulled in so many directions I couldn't tell which way was up and which way was down. Until the very thought of sex made me sick to my stomach.

It was a whirlwind existence that sucked me up and spat me out. I never knew fun could be so stressful. Then one day, I was in an elevator going up to some rooftop party and something snapped in me. I didn't want to be at the party. I hadn't wanted to do the hundreds of things I'd been told to do over those last few months. So why the fuck was I doing them? No one was forcing me. No one had a gun to my head or was holding my firstborn child hostage.

In hindsight, I should have left way earlier. If I'm honest, it was a miracle I managed to step away when I did. Giving up the glitz and glamor of that lifestyle was one of the easiest and hardest things I've ever done. The second I decided I was done, a weight lifted off my shoulders and I could finally breathe again. Then five seconds later, I was clamoring for that drug of fame, recognition, and relevance.

Some people might say it's that weird thing that happens when fame gets to someone's head. I don't know if that's what it was. I only know it took me almost two years to feel like I was a normal person again—and most importantly, be okay with being just another guy on the street.

I stare at my laptop. What the hell am I thinking? After all the effort I put into getting away from that life, why am I even considering jumping back in? I mean, if I want to fuck Sebastian, I'm pretty sure I can convince him to have a fling. We don't need to have cameras there to have sex.

And yet...

I pull up Sebastian's OnlyFans page. There's one video that I've watched a few times now, a "collab" Sebastian did with some guy called Noel. They look like they're friends. Noel teases Sebastian a lot and Sebastian rolls his eyes like he's annoyed and amused at the same time. The level of comfort between them is enticing, enchanting.

The video isn't one of those big studio productions I'm used to. The quality's still there though—good lighting, good angles, decent enough sound to pick out what they're saying to each other. It's intimate and unassuming.

It feels like I'm sitting in the room with them, that I could stand up at any moment and join them.

Sebastian gives Noel a blowjob and he looks exquisite while he's at it. His lips are stretched thin. He's got spittle running down his chin. He's looking up at Noel with a mix of affection and sass.

That's not the way he looked at me over dinner. His gaze was more heated then, more intense, like our attraction is a simmer on the cusp of a boil. If that were me with my cock in Sebastian's mouth, he wouldn't be looking at me with affection and sass. He'd be looking at me with desperation, hunger, need.

My hand drifts to my thickening cock and I grip it through the soft fabric of my sweats. On the screen, Sebastian is on all fours in the middle of the bed. He's angled so the camera can capture the way his back bends and his body arches. He rests his cheek on a pillow and reaches back to pull his ass wide open.

The video cuts to something handheld and we're treated to a close-up of Sebastian's hole. It's twitching in anticipation. A hand appears—Noel's—and he pushes a finger into Sebastian's body.

"Oh, fuck," one of them mutters on the screen. Noel sinks his finger all the way down to the knuckle with zero resistance. Then he does it again with two. Sebastian's hole stretches easily.

The mic on the handheld camera picks up the squelching sound of Noel's fingers as he pumps them in and out of Sebastian's ass. It's raw, unfiltered, obscene. It makes me wish that it were my fingers in Sebastian's body, not Noel's. It makes me wish that other people were as jealous of me as I am of Noel right now.

I reach into my sweats and pull out my cock. I'm leaking pre-cum, enough that I can probably jerk myself off without adding lube.

"Fuck me already," Sebastian says in the video. Noel extracts his fingers and lines up his dick. He's not wearing a condom and the camera captures every second of Noel sliding into Sebastian. The initial resistance, the way Sebastian's hole expands, the way it contracts to suck Noel's cock in. The camera sees every inch of hard flesh, every ridge and vein as they disappear past that ring of muscle.

When Noel bottoms out, my eyes drift shut. I imagine it's my cock in Sebastian's ass. I imagine it's me fucking him bareback. It's me slamming into him, my hips slapping against the back of his thighs. I'm the one wringing those sounds of pleasure from Sebastian's mouth. I'm the one wrecking him, making him come apart.

"Fuck. Yeah, like that. Oh fuck. Right there. Fuck." Sebastian's voice comes through the speakers like he's speaking directly to me. My hand grips tight around my dick as I pump into it with Sebastian's encouragements ringing in my ears. The base of my spine tingles. My balls draw up.

On the screen, Noel pulls out and comes all over Sebastian's ass. Creamy white cum paints Sebastian's skin and holy fucking hell, I want it to be my cum. I want it so badly that my dick explodes like it's trying to do just that. Like if I orgasm hard enough, my cum can somehow transcend space and time and end up on Sebastian's body. It's still pulsing even after my balls are empty, even after my skin has gotten too sensitive to touch.

Goddamn, I haven't come this hard in ages, not even

during the last time I watched this video. My hand is covered in cum. My shirt is splattered with it.

The sound of cries draws my attention back to the video. Noel's got his lips wrapped around Sebastian's cock now, his head bobbing up and down in a loud and messy blowjob. Sebastian gives Noel a warning right before he comes on Noel's tongue. Then Noel crawls up Sebastian's body and feeds his cum back to him.

They kiss each other. Sebastian giggles and Noel smirks. They both turn to the camera and smile at it. It feels like they're asking if I had as much fun as they did. I want to hit replay and watch the video all over again.

I drop my head back on the couch cushions. "Fuck," I mutter.

It isn't just the sex. It's this—the nebulous thing between them on one side of the screen and me on the other, the way they seem to reach through the camera and connect with the viewer. *This* is hot as hell. *This* is something I don't think I've ever experienced when working with the studios. It sounds silly, but it feels like art.

When I compare my career to what I know about Sebastian's, the difference is stark. Mine was about the extracurriculars, the parties, the media, being seen at the right places, with the right people. What Sebastian's doing feels fully grounded in the... whatever you want to call it, the content, the business, the art. He's serious about this, it isn't a game to him. He's made his fans a promise about what they're going to get from him and he's determined to deliver. That mindset comes through in his videos. It's what makes him so relatable, why it feels like you're sitting in the room with him.

Would I be able to do that? That's the question that's

been nagging me since Sebastian walked into the gym with his damned business card. If I strip away all the fancy wrapping, can I do what's at the core of this industry? Can I create erotic content that entertains people, makes them feel good about themselves, makes them happy?

I don't know. But I want to find out.

Maybe I haven't let go of my past as completely as I thought I had. Maybe there's some part of me that wants to give it another shot, one last go, to see what I can do in this new world of content creators shooting porn in their bedrooms. To see if I have what it takes. Sebastian and his friends seem to think I do.

Maybe I owe it to myself to try.

CHAPTER
NINE

SEBASTIAN

Rhys and Hayden are talking about something to do with some movie. I'm not listening to them. I'm bouncing in my chair, eyes glued to the door for Noel to appear any second now. Any second...

I've been vibrating with excitement ever since my dinner with Christian, ever since he asked me to send him more information about a potential collab. I was barely able to sleep last night. I might have gotten to the brunch restaurant twenty minutes early.

I was *this close* to texting everyone last night, but I made myself wait. I wanted to see the reaction on their faces in person. And now Noel, jerk, is late.

"What do you think?"

"Sebastian?"

"Huh?" I drag my eyes from the door to find both Rhys and Hayden watching me with curiosity. "Sorry, what was that?"

"You okay?" Hayden asks.

"You seem really distracted."

"Oh, yeah, no, everything's fine. Do you know where Noel is?" I check the time on my phone. Again. "He's ten minutes late already."

"That's pretty normal for him," Hayden says.

"He's probably not going to show for another ten," Rhys adds.

Yeah, that's not going to work for me. I've waited literally hours. I don't know if I can wait another minute. "I need him here. Now."

"Is something wrong?" Hayden furrows his brow in concern.

"No, no, nothing's wrong. I just have some big news I want to share."

Rhys lights up. "Ooo, what is it?"

"I wanted to wait until Noel gets here so I can tell you all together!"

"Do you want to call him?" Hayden suggests.

I doubt Noel would even pick up if I did.

"Oh! He's here! He's here!" Rhys claps his hands lightly and waves Noel over.

"Finally! What took you so long?" I ask as Noel drops into the last empty chair around our table.

"Am I late?" Noel's still got his sunglasses on and he pushes his fingers under them to rub his eyes.

"Yes, you are. Sebastian has some news he wants to tell us." Rhys is sitting at attention, eyes trained on me.

"Okay, so, you're never going to guess what happened."

"You're moving," Rhys jumps in.

"No, I—"

"You won the lottery." Rhys again.

"No, not that—"

"You met Ryan Murphy at a party and he's going to make you a star."

"Rhys!"

"Sorry, sorry! I wanted to see if I could guess." He shrugs.

"Can you just tell us already?" Noel perches his sunglasses on top of his head and plants both elbows on the table to cradle his face in his hands. He looks a little green around the edges.

"What happened to you?" I reach over to pull one of his hands away. "Are you hungover?"

"No. Maybe. Yes. I had a long night."

"Doing what?" I ask and Noel tugs his wrist out of my grasp.

"Were you out partying?" Rhys asks.

Noel waves his hands in front of his face like we're flies that he can swat away. "No—it's not important. Didn't you have something you wanted to share with the class?" He shoots a glare in my direction, but he looks so miserable, I actually feel sorry for him.

"Are you sure you're okay?"

"Yes, I'm fine. Nothing that some coffee won't cure. Your thing. Go. Talk."

"Okay." I lean forward and gesture for them all to gather in close. Hayden and Rhys shift to the front of their chairs. Noel slumps down in his. "Remember when I told you about Christian? Er… Chris Preacher?"

"The old guy?" Rhys clarifies.

"The guy from Mars Fitness," Hayden says.

"What about him?" Noel deadpans like trying to add

any inflection to his voice is completely beyond him this morning.

"I had dinner with him!" I squeal, I can't help it. I'm still pinching myself over that.

"You did?" Rhys's eyes are as wide as saucers. "And? How was it?"

I sigh. "It was amazing." It was more than amazing. Even if we never end up working together, I'll always treasure that one date we had together. I mean, not that it was a date, but come on, it was kinda like a date, right?

"Wait. Backtrack. How did you end up at dinner with what's-his-name?" Noel's sitting up a bit straighter now too.

"Chris Preacher," I correct him even though I know he knows what Christian's name is. "I asked him if he wanted to have dinner. He said yes. So we went and had dinner."

"Just like that? You just walked up and asked him?" Hayden asks, incredulous.

"Well, sort of." I explain the whole bumping into him incident, and the way he took my arms to steady me, and how we ended up staring into each other's eyes.

"Aw, that's like, a real-life meet cute." Rhys has hearts in his eyes and, you know what, I do too.

"What's a meet cute?" Noel asks, brows furrowed in skepticism.

"You know," Rhys says. "In romcoms, where the two characters have some sort of accident that's kind of awkward, and kind of adorable, and it's love at first sight?"

Noel stares at Rhys like he's speaking a foreign language.

"It's like when two people bump into each other at a

coffee shop, and one of them spills coffee all over the other. Then they offer to buy them another coffee, and it turns into a date," Hayden explains.

He and Rhys and I watch Noel to see if he gets it and... if he does, he's not impressed.

"Okay. So, why is that important?"

"It's not," I say. "What's important is that when we were at dinner, we talked about a collab!"

"Ekk!"

"What did he say?"

"Did he tell you why he quit?"

"I know! He's thinking about it. And no, he didn't." I answer Rhys, Hayden, and Noel in turn.

"So... that's it? You went to dinner?" Noel asks. He's slumped so far down in his chair he looks like he's about to slide off the thing altogether.

"What do you mean 'that's it'? That's like, everything! He's seriously considering it! I sent him all the documentation." Christian even responded to the email saying that he would review it all and get back to me. I might have been obsessively refreshing my inbox ever since.

"Oh god, not the documentation." Noel groans, covering his face with his hands again.

My head snaps around to Noel. "What is that supposed to mean?"

"You sent him all of it?" Rhys is wincing.

"Well, not *all* of it." There were some on-location liability forms I left out because we're most likely just going to film at my apartment.

"You asked him for his emergency contact?" Rhys's wince deepens.

"Yeah, of course I did. It's on the general consent form. I send that to everyone."

Noel peeks at me from between his fingers. "No one wants to give you their emergency contact."

"Why not?" My question is interrupted when a waiter shows up to take our order. He's a chatty one, this waiter, and normally, I wouldn't mind, but we're kind of in the middle of an important conversation.

"Why can't I ask people for their emergency contact?" I ask the second he steps away. "What if something happens during filming? What if we need an ambulance or something? I need to know who to call."

"What could possibly happen?" Noel rolls his eyes. "It's just sex on camera."

"Which can be dangerous if we're not careful," I say. "We put ourselves in rather precarious positions sometimes. And what if there are toys involved?"

"Do you ask random hookups for their emergency contact before having sex?" Noel asks.

Rhys jumps in. "I think what Noel is trying to say, is that it can be a lot." His voice is gentle, like he's telling some kid that their favorite ride at Disney World is closed for repairs.

"What do you mean, 'a lot'?"

"Well, it can be a little intimidating," Rhys says.

I sit back, worry gathering at the back of my mind. Does Christian find it intimidating? Would he say something if he did?

I pick up my phone and scroll to the response he sent me last night.

Thanks for this. I'll take a look and let you know soon.

It sounded pretty innocuous to me when I read it last night. But now that the guys seem to think I'm "a lot", I'm wondering if "let you know soon" is code for "yeah, no thanks." Shit.

"I'm with Sebastian on this one," Hayden says with a shrug. "I think it's smart the way you do it. Better to be overly cautious than get caught unprepared, right?"

Right. Yes. I'm not totally off-base. "Yeah, that's exactly it."

Noel levels a look at Hayden. "Don't you get him started."

Hayden holds up his hands, palms out. "I'm just saying. It's not like there's a shortage of guys who want to work with Sebastian, so obviously not everyone thinks it's too much paperwork."

"Do you know who I put down as my emergency contact when we did our video?" Noel asks me.

"Who?"

"You."

I roll my eyes. I knew I should have reviewed his paperwork more closely. I won't make that mistake again.

"So when do you think you'll hear back?" Rhys asks.

"He didn't say. Just 'soon'." Which could mean... anything really. A couple days? A couple weeks? Never? Ugh, that would be humiliating, getting ghosted by my celebrity crush, not even warranting a polite decline, him just straight up disappearing on me. I'd never be able to go back to Mars again. I couldn't risk running into him and having to figure out how to act all cool.

I mean, there's always the possibility that Christian will come back with an "it's flattering, but..." But he seemed so on board by the end of dinner, like his questions would be about minor details in the contracts, not like he was still on the fence about the whole thing.

More than that, I thought we'd connected. We had chemistry, we shared stuff about ourselves. Those moments when he seemed haunted by something? That was real vulnerability he was showing me. He wouldn't do that if he wasn't planning on going through with the collaboration, right?

"I'm sure he'll respond soon." Hayden gives me an encouraging smile.

I try to return it, but I don't really succeed.

"And if he says no," Noel shrugs dismissively, "then it's his loss."

That drags a real smile out of me. For all his attitude and abrasiveness, Noel is surprisingly supportive when I least expect it.

"Thanks, guys. You're the best." I just hope I don't have to come back to brunch in a couple weeks with my tail between my legs.

Later that day, Christian's email comes through. I open up every attachment and review every page. He's filled out all the documents, signed on all the lines, and with each file that I save onto my computer, my heart beats a little faster. This is happening. He's agreed to it. We're going to shoot a video together.

I save the last file and sit back, staring at the screen, letting the reality of my situation sink in. Then I carefully set my laptop aside, rise to my feet, and freak out a little. There might be some jumping up and down, some screaming into a pillow, some throwing punches into the air. My cheeks hurt with how wide I'm grinning and I feel like I'm going to burst out of my own skin. My apartment isn't large enough to contain me. I need to get out and… I don't know, go running through the streets, shouting at the top of my lungs or something.

I'm going to be working with Chris fucking Preacher!

I've daydreamed about this more times than I can count, but I never truly believed it was possible. Me? Some random camboy filming videos out of his bedroom? Working with someone who's had credits with the largest studios in the industry, who's appeared on countless magazine covers, who's won dozens of awards? He's reduced fans into blubbering messes with nothing more than a smoldering look. He's had people climbing over each other just to see his face, touch his hand, take a picture with him. He's had other performers line up for a chance to get fucked by him.

And now he's going to fuck me. Holy shit.

I sit down heavily on the edge of my bed. He's going to be here, in my tiny little apartment, and we're going to strip down, turn the cameras on, and have sex. Holy. Fucking. Shit.

CHAPTER
TEN

CHRISTIAN

I'm standing on the street outside Sebastian's apartment, waiting for another few minutes to tick by before calling him on the intercom. I'm early and sometimes being too early is just as annoying and inconvenient as being late.

My hands are balled into fists in my pockets and my heart rate is way above resting. Every little sound—every car horn and dog bark and faint strains of music—is blaring in my ears.

I really hope I'm not shooting myself in the foot by agreeing to do this thing with Sebastian. My life is good now. I have a great job. I have great friends. I can't think of a single thing that annoys me enough to do something about it. So why am I trying to mess with what works? Why am I going back to a life I literally ran away from ten years ago? What am I trying to prove?

That I'm not a failure.

I jolt as those words rip through me. It's something I try not to dwell on too often or for too long. Stepping away from porn when I did was not a sign of weakness, it was a sign of strength, I remind myself. I didn't "run away" from anything, I chose a better way of life. More balanced. More sustainable. Healthier. Or so I keep telling myself. And yet...

I haven't felt this animated in ages. Like the air is charged and I keep sparking whenever I run into a stray molecule. Even Donnie looked at me weirdly yesterday and asked if I was seeing someone new.

No, I'm not seeing anyone, no one but Sebastian, that is.

My phone buzzes in my back pocket and when I take it out, it's a reminder that I'm supposed to be at Sebastian's in five minutes. It's too late to back out now. I've already signed all the things, and he's up there waiting for me. Even if I wanted to call a stop to everything, I can't leave him hanging. I press the button for Sebastian's apartment, and his voice immediately comes through the crackly line.

"Hello?"

"Hi, it's Christian."

"Hey! Come on up!"

There's a buzzing sound as the door's locking mechanism turns. The stairs are in the middle of the building and with every step I take, my heart races faster and faster.

Sebastian's standing in his doorway when I get to his floor, and his face lights up when he sees me. He's got that big bright smile on, the one that makes me stagger under its intensity. "Hey! You made it! Any trouble finding the place?"

"No trouble," I say, taking a minute to bask in Sebastian's smile. Warmth settles into my stomach the way it always does when I'm around him.

Sebastian ushers me into his tiny studio apartment. It's the type of shoebox that New York is known for. Kitchen along one side, a small window with a delightful view of a brick wall, barely enough room for a double bed, an armchair, and a tiny desk. He's already got the camera tripods and light boxes set up and I can piece together the angles from all the videos I've watched on his page.

"Can I get you anything? A snack? A drink?"

I had a protein smoothie for breakfast. That was my old routine from back in the day. Can't eat or drink too much before a shoot for fear of a food belly. "Water is fine."

Sebastian pulls a carafe of water out of the fridge and fills a glass. "So, this is it," he says with one of his giggles that makes my skin tingle. He hands me the glass. "Kinda sad compared to what you're used to, I'm guessing."

"No, this feels…" Normal. Ordinary. Average. In a good way. This is a typical New York apartment and we're just two guys about to strip down and fuck. There isn't makeup and wardrobe and a whole crew of people standing around watching. There aren't any lines to memorize or characters I'm supposed to play. I take in a deep breath and when I let it out, my heart rate slows a little. This is… "Nice. It's comfortable. I like it."

Sebastian's smile turns shy and bashful and he drops his gaze, treating me to a view of those long lashes. "Thanks. Um, have a seat." He gestures to the armchair.

It's the same one he shoots videos on and my dick stirs at the memory of him with his leg thrown over the arm, his ass on the edge of the cushion, the shadow of a butt plug between his cheeks. That warmth in my stomach travels down to my balls and I ease carefully into the chair.

I set my bag down on the floor and take a long drink of the cold water.

Sebastian perches on the edge of the bed, his butt barely touching the covers. He looks like he's about to fly off and go bouncing around the room. He's wringing his hands in his lap. He's nervous. Like, way more nervous than I am. Which I don't fully understand since this is something he does all the time. But it's also incredibly endearing and sweet for some reason. It makes me want to go sit next to him, put my arms around him, and soak in all the excess energy he can't contain. It makes me want to pull him into my lap, settle his body against mine, and hold him.

"Thanks for filling out all those forms. I know it was a lot. Sorry about that." He tries to sit farther back on the bed but then scoots forward again.

I shift to the front of the chair and lean my elbow on my knees, bringing us a couple inches closer to each other. "Yeah, sure, no problem."

Sebastian's gaze flits to me, then away. His chest rises and falls a little too fast and his knuckles are white. "Um, did you have any questions or anything? Anything off-limits that you didn't indicate in the forms? Anything about my test results?"

I shake my head. "Nope."

"Okay, good." He nods. He falls silent for a moment like he's not sure what to say next, then points to one of the cameras. "I usually start with an on-camera interview. I'll introduce you, ask a few questions about what you like, what you don't like. Things like that. And then... we get started. Does that sound okay?"

"It sounds wonderful," I say.

"Good." He shoots to his feet. "Great. Awesome."

I stand too and step in close to him. "Hey. Breathe."

He stills immediately. He stares up at me, lips parted, chest almost brushing mine with every inhale. I lift a hand and trail the back of my fingers down his bare arm. He shivers at my touch and my cock fills in response. He smells like vanilla, like chocolate chip cookies, and I bend my head forward for a little more. He sighs and sways toward me, his eyes falling shut.

"Better?" I ask in a whisper.

He nods and his hair brushes against my cheek. "I guess I'm a little nervous."

"I am too."

He lets out a huff of laughter and lifts his gaze to mine. "You? Nervous?"

I quirk my lips into a grin. "It's been a long time since I've done this."

His eyes are wide when he speaks. "But you're Chris Preacher."

I have to chuckle. "That doesn't mean I don't get nervous."

Sebastian takes a minute, like he's letting that new piece of information sink in. Then he nods. "Okay."

"Okay." I force myself to take a step back when all I want to do is get closer. "I assume you've prepped?"

"Uh-huh." Sebastian watches as I toss my bag onto the bed and unzip it.

I've been out of the porn game for a long time, but there are still a few tricks I remember. A protein smoothie for breakfast is one of them. The other is the stuff I pull out of my bag.

Listen, I'm not bragging when I say I'm large. Even for

a porn star. Guys have balked when they realize what they've signed up for, and over the years, I've figured out that the right tools and a lot of patience go a long way.

"I'm on the bigger side," I say, holding up the bottle of lube and the long syringe I dug out from the box under my bed. "This usually makes things go in easier."

Sebastian's brows are furrowed as he stares at the things in my hand. I offer the syringe to him and when he takes it, his jaw drops to the floor.

"Oh my god, is this a syringe?" His eyes bulge. "Wait, is this supposed to go up my ass?"

I shake the bottle of lube. "Yeah."

"Holy shit!" He takes the bottle from me too. "We're injecting lube into my ass?"

"Yeah." I want to laugh at his expression, but I'm also holding my breath because I can't tell how Sebastian feels about this. He's either completely horrified and about to kick me out of his apartment. Or he's going to shuck off his sweats and bend over for me. I really, really hope it's the latter. "Is that okay?"

Sebastian's gaze snaps to mine. "Huh? Oh. Yeah, totally!" He spins around in a circle and pauses. "Um, how exactly do I do this?"

I let my breath out in a *whoosh* and hold out my hand for the supplies again. "I can help, if you'd like." Because yeah, it's kinda awkward trying to use a long syringe to shoot lube up your own ass.

"Can you? That'd be awesome. Thanks! Oh, and do you mind if we film this part?" He's already fiddling with the camera. "It won't make it into the final cut, but I like having some behind-the-scenes footage."

"Sure, no problem." I can't imagine why anyone would want to watch this, but what do I know?

"Cool. Gimme a minute…" He checks the view screen on the DSLR and then hits the record button. "Ready. Where do you want me?" He claps his hands and rubs them together. His eyes are impossibly bright and he's vibrating again, though his energy tilts more toward excited than nervous this time.

I put my hand on his arm and he leans into it with a small sigh. I'm not sure he even knows he's doing that. It's like he's drawn to me as much as I'm drawn to him and together, we're balancing each other out. I turn him toward the bed. "Hands and knees."

Sebastian's in position before I finish speaking, his sweats down around his thighs. I take a moment to load up the syringe and when I look up, I have to bite back a groan. His ass is two round globes that I want to fill my palms with. His balls hang low and heavy between his legs. And nestled right in the middle of his crack is a black knob.

My dick strains against the zipper of my jeans and my stomach clenches with how much I want to climb up behind him and play with that knob. I want to fuck him with it and then I want to take it out and replace it with my cock.

I approach the bed slowly and set my hand on Sebastian's hip. His body melts under my touch and my sudden spike of lust settles itself back down.

"Can I—" I clear my throat and try again. "Can I remove this?" I give the handle of the butt plug a gentle nudge.

Sebastian wiggles his ass and arches his back. "Yeah, go ahead."

I take a deep breath and already I can smell the scent of sex starting to fill the air. I swallow and reach for the plug. It's snug in there, wedged in deep. I work it out of Sebastian and he lets out these soft moans as the plug moves inside him.

We both shudder when I finally wiggle it free. The plug is big, a lot wider and longer than I expected. It's impressive, really, that Sebastian was jumping up and down and all around while wearing the thing. I set it aside and stare at his hole. It's loose and relaxed, the muscle twitching a little like his ass doesn't know what to do when it's not filled.

I run my thumb down his crack and over the wrinkled skin of his hole. I'm going to be in there soon. With my fingers, my tongue, my cock.

"Ready?" I croak.

"Uh-huh." Sebastian's voice is breathy, but he doesn't move an inch.

I lift the tip of the syringe and stifle a groan at how easily it slips inside. Sebastian's only reaction is a quick inhale and a long slow exhale. I feed it all the way in until only the handle and the plunger are visible. Then I pull it out, slowly, as I depress the plunger, making sure all the lube is evenly deposited in Sebastian's body.

The syringe is empty when it pops out and I rub his lower back, his hip. "All done. How's that feel?" My voice is rough and gravelly.

Sebastian's hole clenches around nothing and a drizzle of lube leaks out of him. Before I can stop myself, I scoop it up with my thumb and press it back in. Sebastian makes a soft sound at the back of his throat and my dick throbs. I force myself to turn away and deal with the syringe. My hands aren't entirely steady as I wrap it up in a towel.

Sebastian sits back on his heels and wiggles around a bit. His expression is full of wonder. "Whoa, that's deep."

"Is that okay?" My dick is pulsing in time with my heartbeat.

"Yeah. I mean, it's a bit squishy, but that's the whole point, right?" He looks at me with those bright, shining eyes and it hits me deep in the gut.

"Yeah," I murmur.

Sebastian is beautiful like this. Vibrant and full of life. He's adorable and his awkwardness only adds to his cute factor. He's smart and competent with a touch of nerdy. There's a lot to like about this man. There's a lot *I* like about him.

He tugs his sweats back on. "Ready?" he asks.

I'm suddenly struck with a feeling that I'm going to get way more than I bargained for with this project of ours. And no, I don't feel the least bit ready for it. But when he smiles at me like that…

"Yeah," I say. "I'm ready."

CHAPTER
ELEVEN

SEBASTIAN

"Heya!" I practically shout into the camera. My voice is way too high, but it's kind of hard to speak normally when I've got lube coating half my colon. It doesn't hurt and it's not uncomfortable or anything, it's just... Christian had that syringe really deep in there and... well, does that mean he's going to be that deep inside me too?

God, I really fucking hope so.

"You will not believe who I have here with me today! It is the one, the only, the legendary, Chris Preacher!"

Christian chuckles lightly at my introduction and waves at the camera.

"Chris has been an idol of mine and an inspiration to me for many years. In fact, he was a big part of why I started camming in the first place, so y'all have him to thank for the videos you love to watch. You have no idea how freaking excited I am that Chris has agreed to film this video with me. Like, honestly, *I haven't been able to sleep for days* level of excited."

I turn to Christian who's been watching me with that stare that takes my breath away. It happens again now. It's so easy to fall into the depths of those intense eyes, to lean on him and let him drain the anxiety that's got me all wound up.

He cocks his eyebrow and oh yeah, right, we're filming. I clear my throat. "So, Chris, you've obviously done a lot of scenes with a lot of partners before. Do you have a favorite thing you like to do? Like a position or a sex act or something?"

It's one of the standard questions I ask my scene partners and I warn them about it ahead of time so they're not caught off guard. Most guys just rattle off something like doggy-style or sex in public, a quick answer that's not worth dwelling on, and then we move on.

Christian though, his lips curl into a smoldering grin and his gaze drops to my mouth. My tongue sneaks out, all on its own, to lick my bottom lip and I swear Christian's stare gets hotter.

"I like kissing," he says, so softly that I'm not sure the camera's mic will pick it up.

The words hit me right in the gut. They're like a spark to dry kindling and I'm suddenly burning up. My cock is as hard as steel and my hole quivers with the need to be filled. My mouth has gone dry and the only thing that can quench my thirst is one of those kisses Christian apparently likes so much.

"Kissing, huh?" I say, staring at Christian's mouth.

"Yeah, kissing."

My gaze trails down Christian's body. His wide shoulders, his muscular chest, his flat stomach, and finally his groin where his cock is a massive bulge in his jeans. It strikes me all of a sudden: this is Chris Preacher. The man who's been the object of my dreams for so many years. He's in my apartment. On my bed. I'm going to have his cock in me, his body on top of me. I'm going to know what it's like to kiss him, to taste him.

I reach for him, slowly, like he might vanish if I move too quickly. I trail my fingers down the same path my eyes took, feather-light, just in case this isn't real. Christian moves toward me. I can't move. I can't breathe. I'm caught in Christian's stare, in the way he's devouring me with his eyes. He lifts a single finger to my chin and that's all it takes to keep me exactly where he wants me. Then he proceeds to kiss the life out of me. And fuck, it would be a good way to die.

His tongue darts in and out, teasing, caressing, barely there before it plunges so deep, I have no choice but to suck on it. I groan into it. I've never been kissed like this before. I didn't know it was possible to get kissed like this. Like my mouth is getting fucked by Christian's tongue and all I can do is sit there and take it and moan for more.

Christian presses me onto my back and my hands immediately go to his waist, pulling him down on me. Our cocks meet through layers of jeans and underwear and sweats, which is a shame, but probably for the best. I'm so primed right now that if we were skin to skin, I'd most likely come and the shoot would be over and no one wants that.

I break off the kiss, panting for air, struggling to keep my wits about me. It's so much. It's overwhelming. This is only supposed to be a performance, but it feels like so much more. It feels all-consuming.

Christian trails kisses along my jaw and up to my ear.

He catches the small silver ball of my earring with his teeth. He tugs and it's like there's a string connecting my ear directly to my dick. I jerk under Christian, my hips pushing up to find something to grind against. He pins me with his body, one thigh wedged high against my crotch, then sneaks his arms under me, practically lifting me off the bed to press us closer to each other.

He's everywhere—above me and below me and I'm drowning in him. We need to slow down. We need to draw this out. Or it's going to be the shortest damn video I ever post.

I push against Christian's shoulders and he sits up, giving me some room to breathe. It only lasts for the second it takes for him to strip off his t-shirt, revealing that wide expanse of carefully contoured muscle and two intricate sleeves of tattoos.

Oh god, so much for trying to breathe. He's gorgeous. Like, really fucking gorgeous. It's a thousand times better in person than it is on the screen or in a photograph. It makes me weak in the knees and if I wasn't already flat on my back, the vision of Christian, kneeling there, would send me down.

I push myself up so I can touch him, so I can prove to myself that I'm not hallucinating. I run my palms over the bumps of Christian's abs, over the mounds of his chest. I lean forward to take one of his dusky nipples into my mouth. His skin is taut under my tongue, his muscle jumps under my lips. Christian's fingers weave into my hair as his head falls back with a groan.

I somehow remember to sneak a glance toward the camera, where the view screen is flipped around so I can check our framing without having to get out of bed. What

I see stuns me. Christian looks like he's lost in pleasure. Eyes closed, mouth open, back slightly arched to put himself on full display. I'm below him, lips and tongue worshiping every inch of skin I can reach, hands around the narrow of his waist, holding him to me.

The framing is perfect. We're perfect together. My heart flips over in my chest.

I reach for the button on Christian's jeans. He bends his head forward to watch as I pull the zipper down one tooth at a time. He's wearing black briefs underneath and the fabric is wet. I suck on it, drawing the pre-cum out of the fabric and onto my tongue. It tastes musky and sharp at the same time and my mind fritzes out a little as the scent of it fills my senses.

I hook my fingers under the elastic waistband of his briefs and pull everything down until Christian's cock springs out, practically hitting me in the face. It's huge. Long and thick with bluish-purple veins running under the paper-thin skin. It looks so much bigger in person than it does in his videos. So much longer and thicker, the head more swollen, the veins prominent. It's magnificent.

I need to suck on it. I need to shove it as deep into my throat as it'll go. But first…

I scramble for my phone that's sitting on a pillow and hand it to Christian. "Take this, point it at your dick."

Christian frowns at it for a second before tapping on the screen. I wait for him to give me the go-ahead before diving in.

I wrap my fingers around his cock. It's so hot and heavy and Christian's stomach clenches visibly as I stroke it. I peek up at him, past the phone he's holding with both hands, to his face where he's scowling in concentration.

I stare at him as I lick him. One long lazy stripe from the base of his cock all the way to the tip. I moan when I wrap my lips around the head—it fills my mouth so good. I tease the slit with the tip of my tongue and I'm rewarded with a spurt of pre-cum that I'm quick to drink down.

Christian's dick stretches my jaw wide as I take in inch after inch. I'm not going to be able to get all of it, not from this angle, but I'm going to swallow as much as I possibly can. He's breathing hard, his thighs trembling under my hands. I gaze up the length of him, directly into the phone's camera, and choke myself a little on his cock.

"Fuck, that feels good," he mutters and a thrill rushes through me.

I'm sucking Chris Preacher's cock. It is in my mouth, halfway down my throat, and he likes it. Chris Preacher likes my blowjobs. It's like a badge of honor that I want to wear on my chest. I want to parade the damn thing down the street so everyone knows: Chris Preacher likes my blowjobs.

I choke myself again and whatever I can't get past my lips, I make up with my fist. It's wet and messy and noisy. Christian's pumping a steady stream of pre-cum onto my tongue and I'm desperate to know if his cum tastes as good, as intoxicating, as addicting.

I push him in deep, deep enough to cut off my airway, and I hold him there for as long as I can, sucking and swallowing and basically trying to suffocate myself on his cock. When I finally pull off, I'm so oxygen deprived that my whole body is tingly and the room tilts sideways.

Christian's hand is on my cheek, his fingers brushing through my hair. He doesn't say anything, but there's a look in his eyes that reaches deep into me. It wraps itself around me and cinches tight. I'm caught. I'm trapped. And it feels like it's exactly where I'm meant to be.

Christian sets my phone off to the side and bends down to catch my mouth in another one of those searing kisses. I could spend hours kissing him, willingly lose entire days just to keep kissing him.

I whine when Christian pulls away. I gasp when he grabs my hips and flips me over like I weigh nothing more than a pillow. He shifts behind me and tugs me into position, knees under me, ass pointed toward the camera. Then he spreads me apart.

"Oh god," I groan.

Christian's breath is cool when it blows over my slick hole. I can't help but wriggle in anticipation, in need. He licks me with the tip of his tongue, a light circle around my hole that is just enough to tease and make me cry. He trails his tongue down my taint, then up to my hole again for another circle. Again and again, he does this until I'm wound up tight and gripping the covers, trying not to lose my mind.

When he finally spears his tongue inside, I practically sob in relief. I'm relaxed and open and Christian's tongue goes in with barely any resistance. I shudder at the invasion, at how easily he slips past the ring of muscle and into me.

"Oh god, yes." I tilt my hips, pressing back into Christian's face. I reach behind me and rub my palm over his shortly-shorn hair, holding him in place as I fuck myself on his tongue.

Christian rakes his teeth against my skin, he rubs his beard up and down my crack. It's so good, all the sensations layered one on top of another until I can feel my orgasm building up inside me. It's too soon, too fast, and I reluctantly push Christian away.

"Had enough?" The amusement in Christian's voice sends another shudder through me.

No, I haven't had enough. I haven't had nearly enough.

"I need that cock in me, like, right now." I push myself up and tug on Christian's arm to get him into position.

He arranges himself at the head of the bed, sitting with his legs out in front of him. I pass him the bottle of lube and he squeezes an extra dollop onto his palm. I'm not even sure we need it, to be honest, with the amount of lube he's already squirted into my ass and all the pre-cum he's leaking. He gives himself a couple strokes, then looks up at me. "Ready?"

I nod.

"Come here."

CHRISTIAN

I am sorely out of practice. There was a time when I could fuck all day, balanced in that sweet spot where I'm aroused enough to stay hard, but not too much that I'm on the brink of coming every damn minute.

Today, I've almost blown my load more times than I'd like to admit.

Sebastian holds onto my shoulders as he swings a leg over my lap and straddles me. His lithe body is up close and unfiltered, right in front of my eyes. His face has been the epitome of pure arousal since the moment I put my lips to his. Those dark eyes and long lashes are two deep pools of lust. His lips are rosy and bruised from our kisses. His skin is glowing and I want to drag my tongue over every inch of it.

So I might be out of practice, or it might just be Sebastian. Because I don't remember being this turned on by anyone in a very long time.

I wrap my lube-slicked hand around Sebastian's dick and give it a couple strokes. He gasps and grabs my wrist, squeezing hard as he pants.

"Too much?"

He nods frantically. I guess I'm not the only one on a hair-trigger. I give him another stroke, gentler this time. I can't help myself. His dick is long and slender and about a million times more beautiful in person than it is on a computer screen. And the way it fits in my hand? It feels like it was designed specifically for me.

I take his hand and bring it behind his thigh to my cock. "You lead. Take your time."

He shifts so the tip notches against the entrance to his body and we both pause for a couple breaths. I can already feel the heat of his ass like this, the promise of what's to come. I keep one hand on Sebastian's dick, helping him stay hard with leisurely pulls. The other hand roams wherever I can reach. His thigh, his ass, his back.

Sebastian tries to sink down on me. Nothing happens. He tries again and I can feel him opening up, but it's not enough for me to pop inside.

"Fuck," he mutters.

"It's okay. Go slow. There's no rush." I keep my voice low and trail my lips along his jaw, his neck, his collarbone. Anything I can do to help him relax, to keep him soft and malleable.

Sebastian lets out a frustrated growl. He wants me inside him, he doesn't want to be patient. I can understand, I feel the same way. But we're not going to get where we both want to go if we rush it.

"Shh," I whisper into his ear. "Easy. Relax. Breathe."

I feel Sebastian take a deep inhale and hold it for a

second before letting it back out. Some of the tension in his muscles melt away with the exhale. He tries again.

It works. I pop in. It's hot. It's tight. Almost too tight.

"Oh my god," I groan at the same time as Sebastian gasps and makes a pained sound.

His dick has gone limp in my hand and he drops his forehead down to my shoulder, fingers digging into my arm.

I massage his cock and plant tender, lingering kisses on his ear, down his neck. I stroke him and soothe him and hold him until his body adjusts and the pain passes. It's always the hardest the first time. It'll be easier next time.

Next time.

My hands tighten involuntarily on Sebastian and he whines again, something between pleasure and pain. He buries his face into the crook of my neck and I'm enveloped in him. Sweet and sensual. Sexy and smart. Sebastian is this clash of opposites that shouldn't work, and yet, it does. I don't know if there will ever be a next time for us, but I like the idea of it. I love the idea of it.

"Shh," I murmur. "It's okay. You're doing great."

Sebastian starts to move, rocking gently back and forth, letting gravity pull him down onto me. His thigh muscles are trembling under his weight and I wrap my arm around him to help.

"There you go. That's it."

Sweat has broken out across Sebastian's skin and it runs down the side of his face. I lick up the salty bead, then catch Sebastian's mouth to feed it to him. He moans and sinks down another inch. His dick is hard again and his movements are stronger, surer.

"You're almost there. You can do it."

He slams himself down the last inch and throws his head back with a cry. I press my face against his neck and together we shudder at how amazing it is to be connected like this.

He feels unbelievable, like a furnace-heated vise that's been clamped over my cock. My balls are already drawn up tight and I am on the brink of coming. I manage not to through sheer force of will alone.

"Fuck, you're huge," Sebastian says, stating the obvious with an almost child-like wonder.

I chuckle and squeeze him tighter. "I knew you could take it."

He chuckles too and when we lock eyes, the connection is so intense that it's staggering. My cock pulses inside him and my fingers dig into his flesh. I want to pound into him, drive in so deep there isn't an inch of him I don't touch. I want to kiss him until our lips are raw, until we're breathing air from each other's lungs. I want to leave marks on him with my hands. I want him to be sore for days after. I want to fuck him and make him mine so badly it scares me.

Sebastian kisses me, soft and gentle, and I kiss him back just as tenderly. The kiss drags on and on, wrapping itself around me and tunneling down into me. It consumes me.

Sebastian swallows down my gasp and starts to move, fucking himself on my cock. He goes slowly at first, trying out different angles until he finds one that works for us. Then faster as he falls into the delicious rhythm of two bodies coming together.

My hands are on his ass, pulling his cheeks apart,

helping him up until only the head of my cock is inside him, then pushing him down until I'm buried to the root. His eyes glaze over and his mouth hangs open. There's a drop of sweat clinging to the tip of his nose. He's making these whimpering sounds that grow higher and louder as we fuck.

Sebastian slows, then stills in my arms. We're both panting hard, bodies slick with sweat. The air is heavy with our combined smell. I could come like this. I want to come like this. So deep inside his body that it'll take days for all my cum to leak out.

He lifts himself off me, turns around to face away from me, then lowers himself back into my lap. My cock slides in easily this time and Sebastian lets out a gut-deep groan as I fill him again.

His head falls back onto my shoulder. His sweat-drenched back is plastered to my chest. His feet are planted on either side of my legs and I raise my knees to spread them even wider apart. Positioned like this, the cameras have a clear view of my cock disappearing into Sebastian's hole, and yet it somehow feels more intimate than before.

I can touch him like this. I can pinch and tweak his nipples and trail my hands down his body. I can stroke his cock and palm his balls. Sebastian is languid, draped all over me, and when I thrust my hips up into him, he has no choice but to take it. I get in so deep it feels like I might lose myself in him.

"Yes, yes," Sebastian gasps. "Right there. Oh god, yes."

I pick up speed, fucking up into Sebastian as he tries his best to slam himself down on me. The sound of skin slapping against skin fills the air. Sweat flies off us. We slide down until we're practically flat on the bed.

We don't stop. Sebastian reaches up and turns my chin so we can kiss. It's awkward and sloppy, more teeth than anything else. But it's what pushes me right to the brink and tips me over.

"Fuck," I shout. "I'm going to come." I pull out just in time to start spewing my cum all over Sebastian's balls and dick. Then I shove myself back into Sebastian's ass and ride out the rest of my orgasm in his body.

Sebastian's hand is flying over his cock, rubbing my cum into his sensitive flesh. His other hand is tugging at his balls, then sliding lower to where my cock is still hard inside him. That touch, such a tiny thing, it sets him off and cum rockets out of his cock. It lands in spurts all over his stomach and chest and I even feel some splatter on my chin.

He bears down on me as he comes and that extra stimulation sends an aftershock through me. Or maybe I come again. It feels strong enough for that as my dick twitches and my balls try to turn themselves inside out.

I have stars in my eyes. My body is floating away. Sebastian is heavy on me and I never want to move. This was good. Really good. It was perfect.

Sebastian chuckles and I chuckle too. Then we're both laughing as we disentangle ourselves. He's covered in so much cum, it's hard to believe it was only the two of us in the scene.

"Fuck, I think I'm in love with your cock." Sebastian's eyes are dancing as he smiles at me.

"I think I'm in love with your hole." I smile back.

He drops his gaze and peeks up at me through his lashes. "You're welcome to it anytime."

I lean over to plant one last kiss on his lips. "I may just take you up on that."

SEBASTIAN

I'm surprised my SD cards didn't melt during filming. That's how hot the footage is. I mean, I know it was hot—I was there. But watching back the raw footage gets me so hard that I have to rub one off before I can focus enough to edit the damn thing. Even then, I need several breaks to cool down because—holy shit, yeah.

It's been two days since the shoot and I'm still walking a little weird. If I stop and close my eyes, I can still feel Christian's cock in my ass, the way he stretched me out and filled me. I can feel his big, calloused hands holding me tight, his soft lips grazing my own. I can hear his grunts as he fucked me, how they reverberated through my body.

I haven't done much except lie in bed since he left. That's how dazed and out of it I've been. Honestly, I think Christian might have ruined me for other guys.

And it wasn't just his monster cock.

That scene with Christian was more than good sex. It

was... something else. I don't know how to explain it. The way our naked bodies came together, raw and primal. The connection we had when I looked into his eyes. I've never experienced anything like that before—not with performers I've worked with, not with anyone, period.

I shake my head and hit save a million times before setting my laptop aside so I can stand up and stretch. My muscles protest the movement and I lean into the stinging pain. It's a reminder of what happened, that I did a scene with Chris Preacher.

The thought draws me up short and makes me feel a little icky for some reason. I mean, I *did* do a scene with Chris Preacher and that's like, fucking cool. But to whittle down what we did to such a simple descriptor feels... wrong. It didn't feel like merely a scene, certainly not one between two professionals who are well-versed in having sex on camera. When we were on that bed, when Christian was inside me, I didn't feel like Sebastian Silver and he didn't feel like Chris Preacher. It felt like we were just Sebastian and Christian.

I shake my head again. God, what am I doing? I getting too attached, too emotional about a simple video. I grab my phone and pull up the text thread I have with Noel.

SEBASTIAN

This video is going to blow your mind.

I go searching for a snack in the kitchen and Noel's response is waiting for me when I pick up my phone again.

NOEL

The one with Chris Preacher?

SEBASTIAN

Yeah, it was so fucking hot.

Did he ever tell you why he quit porn?

Fuck you. No, he didn't and I didn't ask.

People are gonna wanna know.

It's none of their fucking business.

Just sayin' *shrug emoji*

I huff and drop my phone onto my bed. It shouldn't matter why Christian quit porn. It's no one's business but his own and he doesn't owe anyone an explanation.

Except, Noel's right. As soon as this video hits the internet, fans and industry people are going to swoop down on us, and the first thing they'll want to know is why Christian's come out of retirement now—with me. We need to be prepared with an answer, even if it's a fake one.

I switch over to the text thread with Christian.

SEBASTIAN

Hey, so… just wanted to check in with you before I post our video.

Three dots immediately pop up on the screen and I'm all bubbly inside knowing that Christian is on the other end of this invisible line.

CHRISTIAN

Sure. I'm done at 7 tonight.

I'm about to suggest a phone call or maybe meeting up,

but the three dots are still bouncing up and down. I never know whether that means someone is actively typing or whether they've got their cursor blinking, waiting for me to respond.

CHRISTIAN

Want to have dinner?

I stare at the words as my heart rate goes through the roof. Do I want to have dinner with Christian? What kind of question is that? Hell, yeah, I do.

SEBASTIAN

I'd love to. Let me know when and where. I'll be there.

CHRISTIAN

How about my place?

Uh... Christian's place? That's like... like we know each other, like we could be friends. The whole of my being gloms on to the idea. I could be friends with Christian, this super hot older man who is nice and kind and the fulfillment of all my wildest dreams. My hands shake a little as I'm tapping out my response.

SEBASTIAN

Yeah, sounds great!!

I hit send and curse. Should I have used two exclamation marks? It's probably too much, right? Overly excited? One would have been enough. Or maybe none because I'm supposed to be professional. Exclamation marks don't scream professional.

CHRISTIAN

Looking forward to it.

See? Christian didn't use any exclamation marks. I drop my head into my hands and groan. Why am I like this? I know that punctuation doesn't matter. Who cares if I used one or two. So what? But my brain can't let it go. Goddamn brain.

There are still a few hours before I need to leave for Christian's and now I'm too worked up to sit down and try to edit some more. So I change into my running gear to work out some of this pent-up anxiety.

I have a set route that takes me through Prospect Park. At about the midpoint mark, I stop for a short social media break—no rest for the entrepreneur, remember? I frame up a selfie and take a dozen before there's one I like.

Taking a break from editing the most epic video with a certain special guest star. New content dropping in a few days!

Two seconds after I hit post, the likes and comments start rolling in. Fans are guessing who the guest star will be and the early favorite is Noel. I smile to myself. It's definitely not Noel and they're definitely not going to be able to guess.

I tuck my phone away and finish the second half of my run. The comments have exploded by the time I get home and I carry that rush of validation through a long, hot shower.

I take the time to brush my teeth too and fuss with my hair, then I pull on my favorite pair of jeans and the olive-green t-shirt that contrasts nicely with my skin. Not that this is a date or anything. But I should look good for a professional meeting too, right?

By the time I'm changed and ready to go, my fans have decided that the guest is either Noel or another popular camboy named Bellamy Blais. They are going to be in for the surprise of a lifetime.

Christian lives a couple subway stops from me and I practically bounce the whole way there. My skin is all tingly and my stomach is all fluttery and I'm vibrating with so much energy I might burst. I'm at Christian's building. I'm going to be in his apartment. This cannot be real.

I hit the buzzer next to his name and nothing happens for a moment. Shit. I'm early—am I too early? Should I press the buzzer again? Should I try texting to let him know I'm downstairs? I double-check the address to make sure I've got the right building.

I'm just about to buzz up again when there's a hum and the door unlocks with a loud click. Christian's door is propped open when I approach and I give it a firm knock before easing it wider.

"Hello?"

"Yeah, come in. I just need a minute."

I slip through the door and shut it behind me. "Sorry, I guess I'm early." I cringe at my own eagerness, at my apparent inability to regulate my enthusiasm. I should have waited downstairs or walked around the block rather than show up before Christian was ready.

"No worries." He comes out of the bedroom and I forget how to breathe. He's wearing a pair of joggers that cling to his hips and are fitted enough to show off how thick his thighs are. The tank top he's wearing leaves his bulging biceps and most of his chest and ribs bare. His hair is darker than normal and he's running a towel over his head like he just got out of the shower.

Probably because he just got out of the shower.

Damn, now I wish I'd shown up even earlier. Maybe I could've caught him in nothing but a towel.

I drag my eyes back up to Christian's face. "Hey." My voice cracks. Goddamn it.

"Hey." Christian's voice is too low to crack and he's smiling at me like he knows where my thoughts have drifted.

"Um." I swallow. "You've got a great place." Not that I would know since I haven't bothered to look at anything but Christian since I set foot inside.

"Thanks. You want something to drink?" Christian disappears into the bathroom for a second then comes back out without the towel. "I've got…" He goes to check the fridge. "Beer and water."

He glances up at me, a little sheepish and the butterflies in my stomach go wild.

"Beer's good."

Christian pulls out two bottles and pops the caps off both. My fingers brush his when he hands one to me and a shiver runs up my arm that has nothing to do with the coolness of the bottle.

"What do you want for dinner? I thought we could order something. There's El Pescador, a really good Mexican place not too far from here."

I take a gulp before answering. "Uh, yeah, sure. I'm good with anything."

Christian nods to the couch. "Grab a seat. I'll send an order through."

I sit on the couch and force myself to actually look around. The apartment is nice—way nicer than mine. Not luxury, but big by New York standards and effortlessly comfortable. The furniture is understated yet stylish. The couch I'm sitting on is large enough to take up almost an entire wall. The TV on the opposite wall is both huge and discreet somehow. The windows look out onto a tree-lined street that's quiet enough that the constant noise of the city is at a minimum.

Christian comes to sit next to me, not close enough that we're touching, but not on the other end of the couch either. He drapes one arm over the back of the cushions and turns toward me.

"I hope you like tacos," he says.

"I love tacos."

He grins and every piece of conversational small talk I've ever learned goes *poof* from my mind. All I can think about is that I've been naked with this man. I've had his cock down my throat and up my ass. We've kissed so deeply that it felt like he was sucking my soul out of my body.

It's suddenly really hot in the apartment.

God, this is… whew. I've worked with a lot of guys over the years. Some really hot guys, some guys I ended up dating for a while. But even with the ones I thought I had a lot of chemistry with, it's never been like this. Like it's hard not to stare. It's hard to keep my hands to myself. It's hard not to crawl into his lap and shove my tongue down his throat again.

Jesus. I shift around, trying to find an angle that doesn't make my cock bulge too obscenely in my jeans.

Christian takes a swig of his beer. "You wanted to talk about the video?"

"Right, yeah, I do. Um, so I think we need to come up with a story."

Christian's brows furrow. "A story?"

"Yeah, because people are going to ask. Like, how did we meet? Why did you agree to film the video with me? Especially since you've been retired for so long."

The more I talk, the deeper Christian's frown gets until he's full-on scowling at the coffee table. Shit, he's not happy. I should've anticipated this. He was so private about why he retired, why wouldn't he be equally private about why he's coming out of retirement.

"Is that, um, okay?" I ask, all the earlier fluttering in my stomach turning into one solid mass.

His gaze snaps to mine but it still takes a few moments for his scowl to dissipate. He takes one of his deep breaths, his chest expanding under the loose fabric of his tank top. "I guess so."

Which sounds a lot more like "no" than "yes."

"I mean, we can just, like, make something up. It doesn't have to be anything elaborate. It doesn't even have to be the truth, if you don't want. It's just better for us to be prepared than be... you know."

He nods even though he's still tense. His hands have curled into fists and he shifts to lean forward and sets his elbows on his knees.

Double shit. I hadn't mentioned the need for a story before we started filming. It's something I should have thought of, but I was so caught up in the excitement of getting to shoot with Christian that it never crossed my mind. It's something he should have factored into his deci-

sion and it's my fault that he didn't have all the information he needed.

"I'm sorry!" I blurt out. He's already signed the
contract, so legally, I have the right to publish the video.
But there's no way in hell I'm doing that if he doesn't want
it out there. The video is going to bring a lot of attention
down on him and the last thing I want is for him to regret
what we did.

It's fine. Even if I'm the only one who ever gets to see
the footage, it'll be worth it. It'll be my little memento, my
souvenir. If that's all I get out of this interlude, then that'll
be enough.

CHAPTER
FOURTEEN

CHRISTIAN

"I'm sorry!"

I snap my head around to find Sebastian halfway to his feet. I stand with him. "What do you have to be sorry for?"

"I should've told you before we filmed that we'd probably have to do this."

I don't really see where he's going with this. "Did you purposefully not tell me?" That doesn't seem to fit with everything else I know about Sebastian.

His eyes grow wide. "No, of course not! I just didn't think of it beforehand. But I was telling my friend about our video and he reminded me that people are going to ask."

Sebastian is wringing his hands in front of him and I take them into mine. Those poor fingers. They don't deserve that kind of treatment. I pry them loose and then drag him back down to the couch.

"Then you have nothing to be sorry for. You can't tell me something you didn't even think of."

"But I *should* have thought of it." The self-recrimination in his voice makes my heart hurt. He's so hard on himself, expects so much of himself. It can't be healthy.

"Sebastian, I *should* have done hundreds of things in my life. No one is perfect."

"I know that. It's just—"

I put my hand on his shoulder, then slide it up so I'm cupping the side of his face. "Hey, no exceptions. No one is perfect, not even you, and that's okay."

He blinks at me for a few seconds, his head turning slightly into my hand. It's all I can do to keep him at arm's length rather than haul him right into my lap. My mind is spinning a little at how quickly he got so worked up. I almost feel like we need a little time out before moving on with our evening.

Sebastian sucks in a breath, holds it, then lets it back out. His shoulders slump. "You're still okay with posting the video?"

"Of course," I say before I actually consider the question. The instant the words leave my mouth, I start second-guessing myself. He's giving me an out here, an off-ramp on this freeway that we're barreling down. I can still have my quiet life with my friends at Mars and my full client list, a life that's comfortable and safe.

I like this life—I do. I could be perfectly content spending the next however-many years I have left with this. But I'll always have that "what if?" hanging over my head, wouldn't I? The possibility of something more that I'll never know if I missed out on.

No, I've come this far already. I have to see it through. "Yes, of course I still want you to post the video."

The relief on Sebastian's face alone is worth it and a tightness I hadn't noticed in my chest eases with his smile.

"Thank you," he says. It's two simple words, but the way he says them, so softly and wearily, it makes me wonder whether there's more going on here than I can see. Whether his getting worked up isn't all that it seems.

My buzzer goes off, giving us the excuse we need to hit reset on the evening. I let the delivery guy up and pull out a few bills as a tip. I set the heavy bag of food on the coffee table, then make a quick trip to the kitchen for plates and a roll of paper towels. I don't know how Sebastian eats his tacos, but usually, I'm lucky if I can get more in my mouth than in my lap.

We take the moment to get ourselves set up, sitting on the floor between the couch and the coffee table. I divvy up the tacos—al pastor, carnitas, pescado, and chorizo—and I'm through my first one when Sebastian breaks the silence.

"So, um…" He peeks at me through his lashes. "Why did you say yes to collaborating with me?"

Ah, back to this. I take my time polishing off the chorizo and wiping my mouth. If he's expecting a clean and easy answer, I'm not sure what to tell him. I don't really know how to explain all the complicated thoughts that led to my decision. Sometimes, it feels like it was more a compulsion than anything else.

"I guess I was curious," I finally say. It's the truth, or at least, as close to the truth as I can get. "Your operation is really different from what I've done in the past. And I liked what I saw on your feed."

Sebastian cocks his head. "You've seen my feed?"

Crap. I hadn't meant for Sebastian to ever find out. In fact, I've been meaning to cancel the subscription, but every time I go to the page, I end up scrolling instead of canceling.

I wince as I answer, "Um, yeah?"

He sets his half-eaten al pastor down and sits up straighter. "My OnlyFans page? As a subscriber?"

I sigh. There's no point in denying it now. He can probably look up my information to confirm it. "Yeah, as a subscriber."

Sebastian's eyes dance as he shifts to his knees. "For how long?"

I cringe at how stalker-ish this makes me look. "Not that long?"

He narrows his eyes at me. "How long is not that long?"

"Since you gave me your card?"

His lips part like he's going to say something, then he closes them again. One corner twitches like he's trying to hold back his grin. "Was it... for research? Like, scoping out a business partner?" he asks, amusement lacing his tone.

I rub the back of my neck. "It was partially that," I admit.

"And the other part?"

"Because..." I clear my throat and shift around on the floor. My joggers are suddenly tight as I think back to all the hours I've spent on his page, scrolling and watching and rewatching. "You've got good content. It's... educational."

Sebastian snickers and the sound turns into a giggle,

setting off the bubbly feeling and the goosebumps over my skin. "Educational?"

"Yeah, you know, I read the articles," I say with a smile and an exaggerated shrug.

He leans forward and lowers his voice into a whisper. "Christian, there are no articles."

"What?" I exclaim. "There aren't? I could've sworn there were."

"Uh-huh." He grins at me and I grin back at him.

God, he's really so damn cute like this. Hands braced on the floor, body angled toward me, dark eyes trained on mine. My gaze drops to his lips where there's the lightest sheen of oil from the food he's eaten. I want to lick it off and see if I can taste which taco it came from. I want to lick into his mouth to see if I can taste Sebastian himself underneath it all.

I tear my gaze away when I realize how close I am to kissing him. Whatever this thing is between us—the off-the-charts chemistry or weird emotional connection—it clearly hasn't worked itself out of our systems after the shoot. I'm still irresistibly drawn to him and from the way Sebastian's blinking the daze from his eyes, he must feel it too.

I pick up a taco and stuff it in my mouth, more for something to do than because I'm hungry. Sebastian does the same.

"So, uh, what do you think about my page?" Sebastian asks after we've each polished off another taco.

"It's, uh…" So fucking addicting I can't make myself cancel my subscription. "It's good."

"Yeah? What's your favorite?" He picks up stray pieces

of lettuce and nibbles on them, but I see him sneaking peeks at me out of the corner of his eye.

"My favorite? I, uh, like the solo videos." I clear my throat and try to adjust myself without Sebastian noticing. "Especially when you've got something up your ass."

Sebastian takes in a silent, open-mouthed breath, his chest expanding wide and fast. His Adam's apple bobs as he peeks at me again. "Why do you like the solo ones?"

I think back to the latest solo video I watched. "It's the way your eyes look," I say, remembering Sebastian's face on the screen. "You look surprised right before you come. Like you didn't expect it to sneak up on you. Or like you're overwhelmed by the sensations."

Sebastian's lips are parted and his tongue slips out to wet them. His breathing is light and shallow now and his eyes are going a little hazy again. "Oh, that's, uh…"

Christ, I really want to kiss him. It wouldn't be difficult. I'd just have to lean over, hold him by the back of the neck and press our lips together. I already know what he's going to do, the way he's going to melt under my touch, the way he'll whimper into my mouth. He wants it too. It's written all over his face, in the way he's looking at me with all that molten heat in his eyes.

Sebastian looks away first this time, dropping his gaze and turning his body away from me. I have to stop myself from reaching for him, from dragging him back toward me.

"I, uh, I have the rough cut of the video done. If you wanted to watch it?" His back is toward me and he's digging into the bag he brought with him.

It takes me a moment to figure out what video he's talking about, that's how far gone I am, how deep I've fallen into this thing. He turns back with his laptop in his hands and a questioning look on his face.

"Uh, yeah, sure." I start clearing the coffee table to make room for his computer. My beer is empty and so is his. "Refill?" I ask, shaking his bottle.

"Yeah, thanks."

I bring the remnants of our dinner to the kitchen and take a moment to gather myself. I don't really understand what's happening between us. It's clearly not normal, not something I've ever experienced with anyone else I've worked with. I'm attracted to Sebastian and it's clear he feels the same way about me. But I've been attracted to hundreds of guys in the past without ever getting this slightly out-of-control desperation for them. It's as if my body's gotten a taste for Sebastian and now it's hooked. It wants more, it needs more, and it has no desire to listen to reason.

I clean up quickly and grab two fresh beers from the fridge. Sebastian's got the video cued up when I get there. We sit on the couch again, laptop on the coffee table in front of us. There's at most an inch of space between us, running from our shoulders down to our knees and the air feels so hot, it should be steam.

The video starts with Sebastian's introduction. I'm sitting next to him on the bed, leaning back, arms braced behind me. I'm not looking at the camera. I'm looking at Sebastian. Seeing myself like that takes me aback. There's heat in my eyes and a longing so potent that the image of it hits me in my gut as I sit on the couch next to him.

I want him. It's written plain as day on my face and anyone with half a clue will be able to feel just how much.

We're kissing, in the video, with plenty of tongue and moaning and heaving chests.

Beside me, Sebastian shifts, his knee bumps mine. I don't move and neither does he.

On the screen, Sebastian's got my dick out and he's looking up at me like I'm a fucking god. My dick is hard and wet with Sebastian's spit and when he chokes on it, I let out a groan that I swear reverberates through the computer and straight into my groin.

My eyes are glued to Sebastian's face on the screen. My heart is ricocheting around in my chest. My dick is swelling in my joggers. Beside me, Sebastian shifts again like he's having trouble getting comfortable. He clears his throat and his breathing picks up speed.

We're both reacting to the video, remembering what it felt like to be there, in the middle of the blowjob. I can remember the wet heat of Sebastian's mouth. The way his tongue felt as it wiggled along the underside of my cock. The pressure on the head when he tried to swallow it.

What does Sebastian remember? Can he feel my cock on his tongue? In his throat? Can he feel how wide his jaw had to stretch to fit me in?

The video cuts to the rimming and the sounds coming through the speakers are obscene. Sebastian's moans and cries echo in my ears. The back of my head tingles with the memory of his hand as he pushes me deeper into his ass. I can taste the clean muskiness of his hole and that ever-present hint of vanilla on his skin. My fingers itch with the need to wrap themselves around his well-toned glutes.

I dare a glance at Sebastian now. His lips are parted, his eyes half-lidded. I'd be surprised if he can even see anything on the screen. The heel of his hand is pressing down on the bulge in his jeans and his hips are tilting like they're trying to come up off the couch.

It's so fucking hot, watching him watch us, seeing how he reacts to things we've already done, seeing him get turned on by the memory of us. I don't care about the rest of the video anymore. It could show the fucking apocalypse for all I care. The real show is right here, beside me, on Sebastian's body.

CHAPTER
FIFTEEN

SEBASTIAN

I should be immune to this footage by now, considering how many times I've already watched it. And yet, there my dick goes, perking up like it's about to get in on the action. My hole clenches, wanting to be stretched again. My lips tingle and my skin breaks out in goosebumps.

Would it be inappropriate to jack off to my own video on my co-star's couch, next to said co-star?

We're at the part where I'm trying and failing to impale myself on Christian's monster cock. The mic was able to pick up on what Christian said to me at the time.

"It's okay. Go slow. Relax. Breathe. Take your time. There's no rush. You lead."

There's something about those encouragements and the way he said them so tenderly that hits me harder than watching his cock disappear into my body. There was so much feeling in his voice and it winds through me and wraps me up like a warm blanket.

He probably says that to all his scene partners.

Does he look that way at all his scene partners too?

My breath hitches in my chest. He's looking at me like that right now, on the couch, instead of watching the video. I can feel the weight of his gaze as it travels from my face down to my crotch and up again. My cock is throbbing in my jeans and I have to press the heel of my hand on it to keep from popping off in my underwear. I don't even try to be inconspicuous about it. Why bother when we both know that the chemistry between us is just as potent now as it was during filming?

The best part—or worst, depending on your point of view—of the video is at the end, when I'm lying on him, back to chest, and he's entering me from below. My body is on full display. Nipples dark, abs contracted, my quad muscles are ropes down my thighs. My dick bounces up and down as Christian fucks me. And the expression on my face is... I swallow now as I stare at myself.

I'm blissed out. I'm high on lust. I look like I'm about to pass out from an overdose of pleasure. I've never seen myself like that before, so deep in the scene that I'm not really aware of the cameras anymore. I'm not acting there. Christian and I are really having sex. I mean, the type of sex I would have with a guy I'm dating and have feelings for.

The video ends and we're quiet. I don't dare move because if I do, I might come in my pants. Christian doesn't move either. His leg is pressed hip to knee against mine. His shoulder is hot against my arm. We weren't touching when the video started, but now that we are, I don't think I'm able to pull away.

"That's, uh... you've got, uh, good editing skills," Christian says, his voice kind of hoarse.

I nod jerkily. "Thanks," I croak.

He clears his throat. "It's uh, a good video."

I nod again. "Yeah, it's gonna be huge."

"You think so?"

I turn at the hint of insecurity I hear in his voice. "Yeah, absolutely."

He reaches up to rub the back of his neck. It's a nervous gesture that I'm starting to recognize. He does it whenever he feels unsure.

"We might break OnlyFans with this video."

His brow furrows. "Break OnlyFans?"

"Yeah, because of all the internet traffic. There's going to be so many people scrambling to watch it that their server won't be able to handle it."

That does not have the effect I intended. Instead of putting him at ease, Christian goes a little green around the edges.

I shift so I'm sitting sideways on the couch, facing him. My knee sinks into the dip in the cushion by his hip and my shin follows the line of his thigh. "I mean, that's a good thing."

His chest expands with his inhale. "Yeah, sure, of course."

"People are going to love it."

His Adam's apple bobs. "Do you think they'll, uh, ask?"

"About why you're coming out of retirement?"

"And why I retired in the first place," he says so softly I wouldn't have heard him if I wasn't sitting so close.

My heart hammers against my ribs. They are going to ask. Of course they are. Fans are always hungry for this type of gossip. I'm exhibit A. "I think they might," I say to soften the blow. "What do you want to say if they do?"

He rubs the back of his neck again and my body moves before I can stop it. I tug at his wrist, then pull his hand into my lap, holding it in both of mine. He talked me back from the edge of an anxiety attack earlier with nothing more than a grounding touch. I have no idea if this is comparable, but I want to try.

"Do you want the truth or..."

"I want whatever you want to tell me."

Noel's ridiculous limp dick explanation pops up in the back of my mind and I squash it as violently as I can. Christian obviously doesn't have a problem getting it up. At least not anymore, not with me.

Christian stares at our hands for a moment, then flexes his fingers so they brush against my wrists, my palms. It's a weird kind of intimacy, us caressing each other's hands like this. It's not a part of the body I think too much about. Hands are utilitarian, they're functional. I don't usually sit around rubbing my hands against someone else's. And yet, it's so comforting, so unguarded that it makes my heart swell with affection.

"I don't really know how to explain it," Christian says.

I wait for him to continue at his own pace while our hands keep moving.

"It was like something snapped one day and I realized I didn't like what I was doing. I hated it. The work, the life, everything. I wanted out." Christian's gaze flicks up to mine. "It sounds stupid, doesn't it? People would kill for that kind of life and I just got tired of it."

The fatigue I hear in his voice makes my heart ache and I grumble silently at Noel. See? Nothing to do with erectile dysfunction. I hook our thumbs together so I can grip his hand tight. "I don't think it's stupid. Maybe you were burnt out."

He nods with a quirk of his lips. "That's one explanation."

I tilt my head. "What's the other?"

"That I couldn't cut it."

My hackles rise. I didn't like it when Noel tried to smear Chris Preacher's good name. Apparently, I don't like it when Christian does it to himself, either.

"Don't say that." I give his hand a shake. "You were the hottest porn star around for years. How is that not being able to cut it?"

The smile he offers me is wry and self-deprecating and I get the sudden urge to kiss it off his face. He is Chris fucking Preacher. He is fan-fucking-tastic. If he needed a break from the constant hustle of the adult entertainment industry, then he deserved one. No one, not even him, is allowed to think poorly of him because of that.

"I'm serious," I say with another shake of his hand when he doesn't immediately agree with me. "You're allowed to have breaks."

"Ten-year-long breaks?"

"Even ten-year-long breaks."

He stares at me for a moment and I stare right back, trying to imbue as much gravitas into my expression as I can. Then he pins me with a serious look.

"If I'm allowed to take ten-year-long breaks, then you're allowed to not think of everything."

A flush rushes up my neck to my cheeks and I drop my chin to my chest. "That's not the same thing," I mutter.

Christian lifts his hand to my chin and raises it back

up. He's leaning toward me now, face only inches away from my own. Our gazes collide and my lips part trying to drag in more air.

"It is the same thing," he says softly before his eyes drop to my mouth.

My tongue sneaks out to lick my lips and I swear he's going to kiss me. His eyes have darkened and his fingers on my jaw have tightened. I want him to kiss me. I want to fall back into his embrace and feel his searing touch again. I want to slide naked against him and rub my cock against his. Fuck, I want that so much.

But he pulls away and drops his hand. The rush of air that comes between us feels frigid against my heated skin. It takes me a moment to blink the haze of lust from my eyes.

By then, Christian's shifted away so we're not touching anymore. I don't like the distance between us. I want us to get closer, not farther from each other. But... I don't know.

There isn't any rule that says we're not allowed to fuck without the cameras on. We're both adults. We can have sex with whomever we want, whenever we want. And clearly, we're both into it.

Except... it *does* feel like we're not allowed. Like we've established ourselves as work colleagues and to act on what we're both clearly feeling would be crossing some invisible line. An arbitrary line that we can erase, sure, but one of us would have to make that first move and neither of us seem to want to.

At least, not yet.

Christian clears his throat. "So, um, when will the video go live?"

I shift a few inches away from him too and grab my

beer from the coffee table. I need something to hold on to so I don't miss his hand so much. "A couple days, I think. I need to finish editing and mastering it."

He nods. "Should I do anything to prepare for it? Like, help promote it somehow?"

My brain kicks into business mode. "I've already teased it a bit on social media. But if you want, we can do a series of promo posts of us doing things together. Like, going for runs or getting drinks and stuff. Fans tend to like it when it looks like we're friends outside of the scene."

Christian seems to consider this. "So, would we actually go do all those things? Or set up a photo shoot?"

The implication of what I've suggested dawns on me and my stomach gets all fluttery at the idea of essentially going on dates with Christian. "Uh, with other guys I've worked with, we actually went out and did those things. Or at least, pretended to? It's easier than trying to set up a photo shoot with props and stuff."

Which would mean seeing Christian at least a handful more times. It would mean getting close to him, touching him, being cutesy with him. It would mean blurring that line that's already kinda hard to make out.

From the way Christian looks at me, I'm pretty sure he's thinking the same thing I am. Can we keep ignoring this thing between us for that long?

His chest expands as he takes in a deep breath. "Okay, sure, let's do that."

Okay, sure, let's do that.

It sounds so innocuous, and yet my stomach feels like it might flutter right out of my body.

"And the story?" Christian asks, plaintively.

"We can tell the truth. You were curious about how the industry's changed."

"And if they ask about why I left in the first place?"

I think about it for a moment. The truth might work for that too. Not, like, the entire truth, but maybe a toned-down, white-washed version of it? "How about, you got fed up with the hectic schedule and wanted a quieter life with a better work-life balance?"

Christian doesn't look convinced.

"That kind of stuff is pretty trendy these days. You know, people quitting big fancy jobs to like, go start a farm or something. You were ahead of the trend."

He smiles and winces at the same time. "Go start a farm?"

"I'm not saying *you* went to start a farm. Just that you wanted a different kind of life and now things have changed and you're going to dip your toe back in."

"And if they ask whether we're going to do anymore?"

The question sends a wave of heat through me. My stomach does more of the fluttering thing and my dick gets nice and hard in my jeans. "Well, um, I guess that's something we can talk about, I mean, if you want."

Christian's gaze trails down my body, leaving me hot and trembling in its wake. When his eyes meet mine again, they're dark. When he speaks again, his voice is a touch gravelly. "Okay, then it sounds like we have a plan."

CHAPTER
SIXTEEN

CHRISTIAN

I'm at Mars when the video goes live. I know it does because Sebastian gave me a heads-up about the timing. And also because my phone proceeds to explode right in the middle of a session with a client. I sneak a peek at it the first couple times it buzzes in my pocket, but then I turn the damn thing off before it burns a hole in my shorts.

After I wave goodbye to my client, I slip into the staff break room behind the front desk and turn my phone on again. It doesn't do anything at first. So maybe it was just that handful of texts I got. But then the floodgates open. My phone literally heats up in my hand as notifications pop up on the screen faster than I can read them.

"Whoa, what's going on there?" Sawyer, the front desk guy asks as he pulls a bottle of water from the fridge.

"Uh, nothing."

"You sure?" He stares at my phone. "Phones don't usually do that on their own."

I throw a glare at him, which he shrugs off as he heads for the door. Donnie comes in as Sawyer's going out.

"Watch out for Christian's phone. It's like a ticking time bomb." Then Sawyer disappears.

Donnie eyes me, then my phone. "What's wrong with your phone?"

"Nothing's wrong with it. I'm just getting a lot of notifications, that's all." I collapse onto the couch in the break room, extending my legs out in front of me.

"Notifications for what?"

"Ugh." I slouch down far enough for my head to rest on the back cushion. I haven't told any of the guys about my foray back into porn. I don't think they'd have a problem with it, it's just... I spent so many years distancing myself from that world and now I'm suddenly going back? I don't know how to explain it to them in a way that doesn't sound ridiculous.

Sebastian seemed to get it though. With minimal actual explanation too. It was a lot easier to tell him than I thought, honestly. But then, things with Sebastian always seem different than with anyone else. Smoother. Effortless.

Donnie sits at the table in the corner with his lunch. He takes a bite out of his wrap and sits back to chew while studying me from across the room. If I'm going to tell any of the guys at Mars, it's going to be him. He's the least likely to give me shit for it.

"I, uh, might've done a thing."

Donnie takes another bite and waits for me to continue.

"A porn thing," I say quietly.

His eyebrows shoot up and he leans forward. "A what thing?"

I can't tell if he heard me and just wants to make my

life difficult or if he really missed what I said. "A porn thing," I say, a little louder.

"You're doing porn again?" Sawyer pops out of freaking nowhere, leaning through the door with a look of glee on his face.

"Oh god." I cover my face with my hands. Now the entire gym is going to know that I've come out of retirement.

"Is it with that Sebastian guy?" Sawyer plops down on the couch next to me.

"Don't you have to watch the desk?" I glare at him.

He shrugs. "Gavin's out there talking to someone right now. So, is it Sebastian?"

How the hell does Sawyer know about Sebastian? Oh right, because Sawyer knows everything about everyone who walks through the gym's front door.

"Sebastian's the guy I saw you with that time, right?" Donnie asks from the table. "Out on the sidewalk?"

"Yes, that's Sebastian. And yes, it's with Sebastian." There's no point in trying to evade their questions. A quick internet search will turn up the answers in about half a second.

"That's so cool. Although, I don't know if I really want to watch someone I know having sex." Sawyer tilts his head like this is actually something worth pondering.

"Then don't," I say.

"Yeah, but like, I should support you, shouldn't I? That's what friends do."

Donnie nods. "I definitely don't want to watch you having sex, but yes, if there's a way to support you without having to do that, let me know."

They're sweet. If wanting to support their porn star

friend slash co-worker is considered sweet. And they haven't asked the questions I've been dreading for days. *Why are you coming out of retirement? Why did you retire in the first place?*

Sawyer's head snaps toward the door and he jumps to his feet with a muttered "Oh shit" before jetting out of the break room. Less than a minute later, Gavin walks in.

"What's this I hear about you doing porn again?"

"That fucking Sawyer." I sit up about to go chase the guy down.

"Sawyer?" Gavin asks, brows furrowed.

"He didn't tell you?" I ask.

"No, it's all over the internet." Gavin holds up his phone to show me Sebastian's OnlyFans page. The preview of our video shows the two of us with our tongues down each other's throats.

I guess Sebastian wasn't exaggerating when he said the video was going to go viral.

"Do we need to hire security?" Gavin asks, grabbing the chair next to Donnie and spinning it around to sit on it backward. "Like, are we going to have mobs of fans showing up at our doors?"

My heart sinks. I don't think we're going to have a crowd control problem, but it's not going to be difficult for people to figure out that I work at Mars. Which means Mars's reputation is going to be affected by all this.

"Shit, I'm sorry."

Gavin cocks an eyebrow. "Wait, do I really need to hire security? I was joking."

"No, not the security." I rub the back of my neck. "I should have run this whole thing by you ahead of time."

Gavin looks even more confused. "What do you mean?"

"I mean, people are going to know that I work here."

"Yeah, so?"

"So people will know that you've got an employee that does porn."

Gavin snorts. "News flash, they already know I've got an employee that does porn."

I wave my hand in circles as if that will get Gavin to understand what I mean. "Yeah, but more people will know now."

"Yeah, and maybe they'll want to sign up for a membership so they can get one-on-one personal training sessions with the employee who does porn." Gavin looks pointedly at me. "You know, like the guy who you did the porn with?"

I hang my head forward. Right. I'd forgotten about Sebastian's free intro session with me. If he hadn't spotted me out on the floor that day, if he hadn't specifically requested me for his one-on-one—my stomach twists at the thought—then I'd never have met him or gotten to know him.

Gavin stands and comes over to give me a hearty slap on the shoulder. "Hey, don't worry about it. Any publicity is good publicity, right?"

"I don't know about that," Donnie says, balling up the paper that was around his wrap. "We don't want to be known for having a mold problem."

Gavin shrugs. "Okay, fine, but in this case, we're good." He gives my shoulder a shake. "Yeah?"

I sigh. "Yeah. Thanks."

Donnie gives me a quick slap on my shoulder too before the two of them leave. Now I'm alone with my phone and the dozens of messages waiting for me.

> **KEITH**
>
> Chris Preacher, you sly dog! Where've you been hiding all these years?

> **ROSS**
>
> Holy shit, Chris, back with a bang, huh?

> **JAMESON**
>
> You back in the game now? Give me a call, I've got the perfect project for you.

I respond to a few of the texts from guys I'm more familiar with and ignore the rest. Then I pull up my text thread with Sebastian.

> **CHRISTIAN**
>
> I guess the video went live this afternoon.

> **SEBASTIAN**
>
> Yeah. I've been getting requests for interviews already.

Crap. Would it have been too much to hope that they would hold off for a bit?

> **SEBASTIAN**
>
> How're you doing?

How am I doing? Fine, I guess. Not like there's any other option. The video is out there, the damage is done. All I can do is go on with my life and hope I haven't made a big fucking mistake.

CHRISTIAN

Fine.

SEBASTIAN

You sure?

Yeah, I'm sure.

Okay. We still on for tomorrow?

Still on for tomorrow.

The three little dots are still bouncing when Sawyer pokes his head into the room again. "Hey, your next client's here."

"Thanks, Sawyer."

Sebastian sends back a string of emojis that I assume means he's looking forward to our first "date". I turn my phone off again and slide it back into my pocket. When I walk out, I realize I've got a smile on my face.

Because I'm seeing Sebastian tomorrow? Or because of all these people coming out of the woodwork? I don't know—maybe both. But the air feels like it's crackling with electricity again.

I meet my two o'clock client outside the locker room and bring him over to the mats for the warm-up. It feels like all eyes in the gym are on me, watching me, and it makes me stand up a little straighter, puff my chest out a little wider.

"You have a good night last night, Christian?" my client asks. "You look like you're glowing."

I chuckle and rub the back of my neck. "No, it's nothing like that."

"You sure?" He gives me a knowing smile and I have to wonder if he's seen the video too.

I nod and point him toward the free weights. "Yeah, but thanks for asking."

CHAPTER
SEVENTEEN

SEBASTIAN

I'm in the middle of stretching when Christian finds me in Prospect Park for our first official promotional outing. Who knew something as simple as a moisture wick t-shirt and gym shorts could look so good on a guy? But then, Christian could probably wear rags and I'd think he was hot.

"Hey," he says as he approaches with that heated stare that always manages to take my breath away.

"Hey," I reply. I know I'm grinning wildly, but I can't help myself. My body automatically reacts whenever I'm within proximity of him. I break out into a smile, I forget to breathe, and want stirs in my groin. Honestly? I don't hate it. I just wish I could act on it. Today, I might be able to.

"I have to warn you," Christian says as he joins me in a pre-run stretch. "I don't run much. I'm not very fast."

"That's fine. You set the pace. But before we get started…" I pull out my phone.

Christian chuckles. "Already?"

"Welcome to the life of a camboy. Document everything." I sidle up close to him and hold my phone out to snap a few selfies.

"Document everything," Christian repeats with laughter in his voice. "That should be your personal motto."

I gasp exaggeratedly then narrow my eyes at him. Giddy happiness skitters over me at his teasing. "Have you been talking to my friends?"

"No, should I?"

"No, you absolutely should not!"

"Why's that?"

I roll my eyes and huff. "They think I'm obsessed with documentation."

Christian cocks an eyebrow and tilts his head. "I might have to agree with them."

I give him a shove and he goes absolutely nowhere, but I don't mind—I'll take any excuse to touch him. "Shut up."

Christian finishes up his warm-up while I post a photo to my feed.

Just going for a run with this legend. NBD.

The likes start coming in before I can even put my phone away. Fans have gone wild over our video. I've spent every spare second refreshing my dashboard, watching as the numbers tick up and up and up. I did some quick calculations this morning and had to swallow down a sob of grateful relief. This is going to be my most successful month ever, like, over the course of my entire freaking career. It feels like I've broken past some invisible ceiling and leveled up.

I'm going to be able to upgrade some camera equipment and add a few extra toys to my arsenal. If I can find a way to keep all these subscribers, I might even be able to move to a bigger apartment.

"Ready?" Christian asks.

"Yep." We set off at a leisurely pace, winding through the park. I wait until we settle into the familiar left-right, left-right rhythm of jogging before speaking. "So, I've been fielding interview requests."

"Oh right, you mentioned that."

"They want to talk to us together. How do you feel about that?" I'd originally assumed I'd handle any media inquiries, but every single industry outlet is more interested in Chris Preacher than they are in boring ol' Sebastian Silver. I don't blame them. I would be too.

"Uh, okay, I guess?"

I sneak a look over at Christian and he doesn't look thrilled with the idea. In fact, his scowl is deepening with every stride we take.

"You don't have to, you know. I can handle them on my own. Or we can say we're only answering questions via email rather than on the phone or with in-person interviews."

We step off the path to jog around a couple of walking pedestrians.

"We can do that? Just over email?" Christian asks when we're side by side again.

"Yeah, of course. I can write it up and send it to you for review. Most of their questions are going to be the same anyway, so once we have one set done, it should be mostly copy and paste."

Christian turns to look at me and almost runs into a bench. I push him out of the bench's way and we go stumbling off onto the grass. I end up in his arms, hands on his chest as he holds me to him.

"You okay?" I ask. My voice is breathy, because of Christian's close call or because there's an inch of air between our lips, I couldn't say.

"Yeah, sorry, I got distracted." He gazes down at me, like I'm the one who distracted him. "You're pretty incredible, you know that?"

I'm already warm from the run and warm from being so close to Christian, but heat flashes across my cheeks. A strangled chuckle escapes my throat. "What makes you say that?"

Christian's arms tighten around me. "Because you are." His voice is so low it's practically a growl and it reverberates from his chest through my whole body. "Filming, editing, distribution, social media, public relations and you're sweet and sexy on top of that? Is there anything you can't do?"

I stand there, stunned. His words filter through my ears and into my brain. Yeah, sure I do all those things, but only passably well. I'm self-taught. I manage. I'm faking it most of the time. The way he says it, the way he puts it all together, it feels like he's describing someone else. Someone who has their shit together, someone who knows what the hell they're doing.

Because, me? Most days I barely feel like an adult.

"There's plenty I can't do," I say with a dismissive half-smirk and an eye-roll.

Christian cocks his head. "Sebastian," he says in a scolding tone.

I don't know what he wants me to say. It's true. There are plenty of things that I should be doing, but I'm not. There are plenty of things I don't know how to do or could do better. There are so many people out there who are more successful than I'll ever be, who have more subscribers than I do, who make more money than I do. I'm not at the bottom of the ladder, but I'm certainly nowhere near the top. I'm solidly in the middle of the pack and even if this video with Christian bumps me up a few rungs, there is still so much more to climb.

"You need to stop with the negative self-talk."

My smirk fades as Christian's words slice through me. They peel me open and all my guts spill out onto the floor faster than I can shove them back in. It's the stuff that no one's seen before, the stuff that I do my best to pretend doesn't exist. My stress, my worry, my anxiety. My need to be better, to be the best, to be perfect. My fear that I'll never live up to my own standards, let alone someone else's. My fear that no matter how hard I try, I'll never measure up.

My eyes prickle with tears and my lungs seize up. I try to push away from Christian, but his arms have turned into bands of steel, dragging me closer. So I collapse into him, forehead on his shoulder so he can't see the horror that must be written all over my face.

How did he know? How could he tell? My mask is normally so finely tuned that no one—not even Noel and the guys—can see past it. I've known Christian for, what, a few weeks, and he's managed to dissect me right down to the bone.

"Hey, Sebastian. I'm sorry. I didn't mean to upset you." He's got one hand carding through my hair and the other rubbing circles across my back.

God, he must think I'm a nut job, freaking out on him in the middle of the park because he tried to compliment me. He guides me around to the bench he almost ran into and we sit down, his arm still tight around my shoulders.

Only then do I realize I'm shaking, like during one of my anxiety attacks, but also not. It's hard to move, hard to breathe, yes, but there's no heavy sense of dread that ratchets up the terror inside me. This feels more like a breaking down than a bracing for impact.

And unlike my anxiety attacks, it doesn't take me long to pull myself together. I sniffle, swipe at the few stray tears that managed to sneak past my lashes, and chance a peek up at Christian.

I don't understand the look on his face. It's dark and intense, like he's angry, but also concerned and a little tortured. He cups my cheek and tilts my head up so he can study my face.

"I'm sorry," he whispers and the depth of emotion in his voice makes me all teary-eyed again.

"You don't have to be sorry. I'm just... a mess."

Christian scowls and I wince when I realize I did that negative self-talk thing again.

"You're not a mess. And even if you were, there's nothing wrong with that," he says it so sternly and I want to believe him so badly, but...

"It doesn't feel that way."

Christian's expression darkens even more. "Well, it's true."

If only it were so easy to believe, to take whatever

Christian says and stuff it into my heart without my anxiety constantly picking at it, threatening to throw it out. "How do you know that?"

Christian waits for me to meet his gaze before speaking. "Because I see you. I see all the work you're doing and how hard you are on yourself. I see how diligent you are and how much you keep pushing yourself to do more and be better. And when I hear you downplay how amazing you are, how much you've accomplished, it…"

Something comes over Christian's face and it softens to a tender expression that makes my heart swell.

"It bothers me when you say negative things about yourself. Because they're not true. And… I don't like it."

I don't know how to respond to that. I'm not even sure I know what it means. But my heart expands in my chest until it's lodged up in my throat and threatening to burst out of my body.

No one's ever said anything like that to me. No one's ever cared about what I think about myself. What does it mean that Christian does?

I jump when my phone buzzes where it's strapped to my arm. I pull it out to find a bunch of texts from the guys.

RHYS

Sebby! Congrats!!

HAYDEN

Really happy for you, dude!

NOEL

Nice job on the nomination.

"Is everything okay?" Christian asks.

I duck my head as my cheeks heat up. "Uh, yeah, it's nothing. They're just congratulating me."

Christian cocks an eyebrow. "Oh? For what?"

I slide my phone back into my armband, texts unanswered. "Um, for the Grabby Awards. I kinda got nominated for one."

"What?" Christian shifts to the edge of his seat. "That's amazing. Twice in a row?"

It takes a second for me to clue in on what he's saying. "Oh, right, yeah, I was nominated last year too."

Christian puts his finger under my chin to lift my gaze to his. "Hey, see? They wouldn't nominate you if you weren't someone important in the industry."

I want to say that all sorts of unimportant people get nominated all the time. I want to point out that I didn't win last year. But I bite my tongue because I can see Christian daring me to contradict him. I nod silently instead.

"Congratulations, Sebastian."

"Thank you." Which reminds me that I'm allowed to bring a guest. I twist my fingers together in my lap and suck in a breath. If I don't ask now, I might not work up the courage to ask again. "So, um, the show is going to be in Chicago this year, and um, I was wondering if you might be interested in, I don't know, coming with me?"

Christian blinks at me. He opens his mouth, but nothing comes out.

"I mean, just as a friend, of course," I rush to say. "I get a plus one and I figured it'd be good publicity for our video and all that. But if you don't want to, that's totally cool. I know you don't want to be too visible anyway. So yeah, sorry, it's fine."

Christian's smiling at me as I babble on, the corners of his eyes crinkling in amusement. "Done?"

"Um, yeah."

"I'd love to go to the Grabby Awards with you."

I gasp. "Really?"

That soft and tender expression comes over his face again. "Of course. With you? Anytime."

CHAPTER
EIGHTEEN

CHRISTIAN

The restaurant Sebastian picked gives me serious date vibes, which, you know what, I'm completely on board for. After our little heart-to-heart on the bench in the park the other day, I'm definitely feeling some kind of way about Sebastian and I'd bet a month's worth of client tips that he feels the same way.

He's so damn hard on himself when he has all the reasons to be proud of what he's accomplished. Seeing him talk about himself like that, like he isn't one of the most impressive people I've ever met, it grates at me. Like I told him, I don't like it. No one has the right to disparage him and his achievements—not even himself.

Sebastian sent over the media queries last night. He compiled a huge list of questions and wrote up a short paragraph to respond to each. I had to chuckle while reading it—how could anyone question their own competence when they can whip up something like that in one afternoon?

The overarching theme of the questions were: where has Chris Preacher been all these years? Why did he leave? Why is he coming back? And reading through Sebastian's responses made me realize something. Sebastian and I are a lot alike—we're both really good at shortchanging ourselves. My reasons for getting back into the game, how I second-guessed my decision over and over again. It's that inner self-doubt that we all have and I've let it push me around a lot recently.

I wanted to prove to myself that I could perform again, that I wasn't this old, washed-up has-been. I wanted one last taste of fame and glory, of the accolades and the public validation. I wanted to stroke my ego again. All for the same reason that Sebastian is so self-deprecating. We've just compensated in different ways.

The host at the front of the restaurant waves me through and I find Sebastian at a little table in the corner. The lighting in here is dim, with candles and flowers in the middle of each table. Most of the diners are in pairs, all hunched over and whispering to each other like no one else in the world exists.

Sebastian stands as I approach. He's wearing a pair of slacks with a dark blue, short-sleeved button-down that shows off the tapered upside-down triangle of his body. I pull him into a hug and close my eyes to savor the shape of him against me.

"Hey," I whisper into his ear.

"Hey," he whispers back.

I trail my hand down his arm as we pull away from each other, and our fingers catch each other's as we take our seats again. My knees bump against his under the too-small table, but I don't mind. I just hook my ankles around his and flatten our palms together.

He gazes are our hands and his lips part. When his eyes meet mine, my heart skips a beat. I don't know whether we'll ever shoot another video together. I don't think I care either way. But I do know that I want to take Sebastian to bed again. I want to kiss him everywhere and lick every inch of his skin. I want to sink into his body and feel him clench around me. I want to watch his eyes as he comes on my cock. I want to see that look of wonder and surprise as his pleasure overtakes him. Then I want to hold him afterward and bask in the way our bodies come together so perfectly.

"You keep looking at me that way and I might burst into flames."

If he meant that as a discouragement, it's not going to work. "What if I want you in flames?"

Sebastian's tongue sneaks out to wet his lips. "Christian…"

"Hmm?"

He swallows and sucks in a breath like the air has suddenly gone a little thin.

Someone clears his throat next to our table and I reluctantly pull my gaze away from Sebastian to find a waiter standing there, a pad of paper in hand.

"Oh!" Sebastian extricates his hand from mine and fumbles with the menu. "Sorry, can you give us a couple more minutes? Sorry about that."

"No problem. Take your time."

"Um…" Sebastian stares at the menu, eyes darting back and forth so quickly I doubt he's actually reading anything. "I don't know what's good here."

"Do you want to ask the waiter to come back and give us recommendations?"

"Huh? Oh, no, that's okay. I'll just, uh, have the lasagna, I think." He reaches for his glass of water and downs half of it in one go. "It's really hot in here, isn't it?"

It is warm, but I think that has more to do with us than the restaurant's temperature settings.

"So, uh, did you get a chance to look at the questions I sent over?" Sebastian asks. He's very deliberately not meeting my gaze and that's fine, considering how combustible we are when we're within proximity of each other, it's probably safer that way if we want to make it through the entire dinner.

"I did. It looks great."

"Anything you want to change?"

I shake my head. "Like always, you've got it covered."

I can see his blush in the dim lighting of the restaurant, which means he must be blushing hard.

"Okay, cool. I'll start responding to the inquiries tomorrow then."

"Sounds good."

"Sounds good. I mean, yeah, cool. Thanks."

"Sebastian." I hold out my hand to him.

He stares at it for a moment before setting his in mine again.

"Relax. Breathe."

He does that breathing thing I've seen him do a few times now, where he takes a deep breath, holds it, then lets it out slowly. "Sorry. I can get a little…" He waves his other hand in the air like I'm supposed to know what that means.

"Yeah?"

He sighs and some of that frenetic energy seeps out of him. "Yeah. It's this thing I have." He peeks up at me through his lashes, then drops his gaze to the table again.

"A thing?"

"Anxiety. I get anxiety attacks sometimes."

I sit up straighter and my hand tightens around his. "Oh, did you just…?"

"This? Oh no, this is normal everyday background anxiety," he chuckles like it's no big deal. "But yeah, it can get bad. I have medication for when that happens."

I can't say I'm surprised. With how tightly wound Sebastian is all the time, I can see how it can spiral out-of-control. "How often does it happen?"

"Uh, it depends?" He starts tracing patterns in my palm and I lay my hand flat on the table to be his canvas. "More often when I'm stressed. Sometimes I go for months without one and then I'll get like three in a row."

The waiter comes back to interrupt us again. Sebastian orders his lasagna and I get a grilled fish. Then I go back to our conversation because this feels like an important part of who Sebastian is, and I want to know everything there is to know about him.

"What causes it to happen more often?"

"You mean triggers?" Sebastian shrugs. "Could be any random thing. That's what sucks about it. If there was a finite list of triggers, at least I'd know to avoid them. It can be something someone says, or something I read, or something I've let myself dwell on for too long. It's like getting trapped in this spiral, and every thought leads to something worse, and there's no way out. It paralyzes me. Like, physically. And… yeah."

I bring his hand to my lips and kiss his palm, my heart

aching for him. I want to strip all that anxiety away like they're barnacles clinging to his skin. I want to wrap him up so they can't get to him again. "Is there anything that helps?"

He rubs his thumb against my cheek, through the short stubble of my beard and I hum at the tingling sensation it sends through me.

"This helps," he says softly.

"This?" I kiss his palm again and it draws the sweetest smile from him.

"Stuff that pulls me out of my own head. So yeah, you, when you touch me, it's grounding."

"Hmm." If touching him keeps the anxiety at bay, then I'll happily follow him around every day groping him.

"You must think I'm crazy." He ducks his head.

"Why would I think that?"

"Because..." He gestures to himself. "I'm kinda crazy."

"Sebastian," I warn him. He knows I don't like it when he speaks negatively about himself, and I'm not about to let him get away with it.

"No, I'm serious." He's drawing patterns on my hand again, wandering up my wrist this time to the inside of my forearm. "Some people are trying to reclaim the word 'crazy.' Like they did with 'queer.' Like, yeah, I'm crazy, I'm proud of it, so what?"

My eyebrows are halfway up my forehead. "Oh. Is that... how you describe yourself?"

He shrugs. "I don't know. But I know I'm not normal."

"Hey." I reach across the table and tap his chin so he's looking at me. "Normal's overrated."

The grin he gives me fills me with so much warmth and affection that I can't do anything but sit there and stare at him for several beats. He's gorgeous. Smart and sexy and not afraid to be vulnerable. He doesn't seem real sometimes. Like how is it possible for someone to be all the good things in the world wrapped up in such a beautiful package?

Sebastian flips my hand so it's palm down and he trails his finger up my arm. "Tell me about your tattoos?"

I glance at the flower on my forearm that he's tracing. "The peonies were my mom's favorites."

His gaze flicks up to mine. "Were?"

A familiar melancholy washes through me. "Yeah, she's passed. So is my dad. They had me when they were in their forties and then they both got sick when I was in my twenties."

Sebastian draws his hand back down to intertwine his fingers with mine. "Oh my god, I'm so sorry. You were close with them?"

I nod. "Yeah. My mom used to put me to work in her garden." I take Sebastian's hand and bring it to the vintage cars on my other arm. "My dad owned a garage and he would put me to work there too." I laugh at the memories. "I basically worked from the time I could walk on my own two feet."

"It must've been hard to lose them," Sebastian says, tracing the gear just under my elbow.

"Yeah, it was. But they were both sick for a long time, so… I threw myself into porn after. It paid well, it was fun, and it wasn't like I had anyone who would disapprove."

Sebastian's finger pauses on the stylized version of the Pink Floyd album logo with a triangle and streaks of rainbow colors. "Pride."

"Hmm." I lift my arm to show the silhouette of two men kissing on the back of my biceps. "And here."

"What's this?" He points to a muddy-looking black splotch.

"Oh god," I groan. "That's supposed to be our family cat from when I was a kid."

"That's a cat?" Sebastian pulls my arm toward him to get a closer look.

"Yeah, it's one of the first tattoos I got. A piece of advice if you're ever getting tattooed—don't go to the discount place."

Sebastian snickers and giggles, and a delightful shiver runs up my spine at the bubbly sound.

"Right. Avoid the ninety-nine-cent tattoo shop."

"And any two-for-one deals."

"Would you get any more?"

I'm about to say no, but something stops me. "I don't know. Maybe. If there's something special I want to remember. Or someone."

Sebastian's lips part and he takes a sharp inhale. He knows I'm talking about him. That should scare me, but it doesn't. The idea is oddly appealing, carrying around something of his, something that reminds me of him, on my body, having him with me forever... I think I want that. I'm pretty sure I want that.

"I don't know," I say again. "We'll see. Maybe someday."

CHAPTER
NINETEEN

SEBASTIAN

#Chastian is the couple's name that fans have bestowed upon us. I don't love it, but who am I to object. Trending hashtags are golden and let me tell you, #Chastian is trending.

The video is still raking in the subscriptions and the views are through the roof. Every time I post another photo of me and Christian together, we get another spike in numbers. The post from our completely platonic and yet utterly romantic dinner. When we went to get frozen yogurt, the mirror selfie we took surreptitiously in the Mars locker room, the afternoon we spent hanging out on the grass in the park.

Fans are eating it up and clambering for more. I've been updating my spreadsheets every single day just to watch those line graphs climb higher and higher. I'm blown away, honestly, by the response we've had. It's bigger than anything I could have imagined, anything I ever dreamed for myself. My goal had always been to make a living, pay my bills, and be comfortable. But this has me thinking, it has me looking to the stars for what might be possible, what might be next.

And it's all because of Christian.

We've talked a lot over the past couple weeks. Like, so much. About everything. His memories of his parents. My family up in Connecticut who's been surprisingly okay with my unconventional profession of choice. Christian's past experience in the industry and how it compares to mine. What I want my future to look like, and what he wants his to look like. I've never talked this much with anyone in my life—not family, not friends, not boyfriends. It feels like we'll never run out of things to talk about.

Which is why I'm on my phone texting with Christian rather than paying attention to the guys at brunch.

"Hellooo???" Rhys wiggles his fingers in front of my face.

I drop my phone into my lap and cover it with a napkin as if they don't all know it's there. "Huh? What?"

"Don't bother." Noel shakes his head. "He's in love."

I scowl at him. "What are you talking about?"

"You and Chris Preacher. You're in love."

"I'm not in love." Guilt wells up inside me the second those words leave my mouth. I don't know if I'm "in love" with Christian, but I certainly feel something for him—something more than the infatuation I had when I was younger, more than the crush I developed when I first met him.

We get along well. We have explosive chemistry. I can't go more than a few hours without checking in with him. Is this love? Or is this a comfortable pattern we've fallen into for the sake of public appearances?

"Are you sure?" Noel cocks an eyebrow at me.

It's on the tip of my tongue to protest again, except I'm *not* sure. How much of this relationship we've created is an act we're performing for the fans and how much of it is reality?

"Wow, you've got it really bad," Noel smirks at me.

"Shut up," I throw back at him.

"Are you going to do another collab?" Hayden's question brings me up short and an unwelcome churning starts in my stomach.

I'm the type of person who likes to stay two or three steps ahead. My calendar usually gets booked up weeks and months in advance. Right now, though, I don't have any new collabs—with anyone—on my schedule. I feel like I'm at a turning point in my career and my options are to go back to what I was doing before or... something else I haven't quite been able to define. All those solo videos, all the collabs with the guys I've worked with in the past, they feel like they're behind me and I don't want to go backward. Except I don't know what the alternative is. More Christian, I suppose. But how?

"I don't know," I admit, spinning my mimosa glass in circles by its stem. "We haven't talked about it."

"Why not?" Rhys asks. "You two are hot right now. You should take advantage of that."

Rhys is right. If I'd shot the video with anyone else, I wouldn't have hesitated to propose a follow-up. But Christian isn't like anyone else I've worked with. Christian is special, and our whole situation has become a lot more complicated than I anticipated. "Our agreement was only for one video. I don't know if he'd be willing to do another."

"You should ask him," Hayden says.

"Yeah…" I don't want to though. I don't want to put too much pressure on him and end up pushing him away. I want to keep seeing him, keep being friends with him—or whatever the heck we've become to one another. I don't want to put this delicate new relationship in jeopardy by asking for more.

"He's in love." Noel gives me a poke in the arm that I swat away. "And we all know you shouldn't mix business with pleasure."

I flinch because that's what it boils down to, isn't it? More videos and more money or these feelings I have for Christian that look suspiciously like love. Wanting both feels a little selfish, and everyone knows that it rarely works out.

Rhys looks at Noel, then back at me. "Wait, you're serious? You and Chris Preacher are dating?"

"No, we're not dating." There's too much vehemence in my voice for anyone to believe me. "And I didn't say we weren't going to do another video, just that it hasn't come up yet."

"I thought all that hanging out was for social media promo," Hayden says.

"It *is* for social media promo!"

Rhys puts both hands over his heart. "Aw… it's a workplace romance."

"Guys, stop it," I bite out. "There's nothing going on between me and Christian."

Around the table, three pairs of eyes stare in surprise at my outburst. I take a deep breath and hold. Then let it out and hold. "Can we talk about something else?"

"Yeah, sure," Hayden says.

"Of course, Sebby." Rhys shoots me an apologetic look.

After brunch, I head directly to Mars. My anxiety is up, creeping in around the edges of my mind. My hands are unsteady and tingling with numbness. It feels like a vise is oh-so-slowly tightening around my chest.

Christian is still with a client when I get there, so I stiffly lower myself into a chair by the juice bar. He shouldn't be long. He'll come find me when he's done. I just need to sit and breathe and wait.

"Hey, you're Sebastian, right?"

My head snaps up to find a guy wearing a Mars t-shirt standing above me.

Fuck. I really don't want to talk to anyone right now, not when I can barely hear over the sound of my heartbeat in my ears.

"Uh, yeah?"

"Awesome. I'm Sawyer." He points his thumb over his shoulder toward the reception area. "I work the front desk on evenings and weekends."

I nod and force my lips into an approximation of a smile. "Nice to meet you."

Sawyer helps himself to the chair on the other side of the small coffeeshop sized table. Goddamn it.

"I started following you on Instagram. I love the posts of you and Christian. Bro, you guys are so cute."

"Thanks."

"You been doing the camming thing for long? Seems like one of those things that's easy to get into but hard to actually do well, you know? Like, I bet there are thousands of guys posting nudes on OnlyFans, but would I want to pay for any of them? Eh." Sawyer shrugs. He doesn't seem to be in a hurry to leave, but then, he doesn't seem to need me to hold up my side of the conversation either.

"Yeah," I murmur and let him continue blabbering.

"Man, I don't think I could do it, though. You need to be like, super confident in your body, right? I mean, I work out, obviously, but doesn't the camera add ten pounds or whatever?"

"I guess."

"There are probably tricks, though, right? Like lighting and angles and photoshop? Although…" He leans to the side to give me a once-over. "You look pretty much the same in real life." He gives me a smoldering look and a flirty smile.

Under other circumstances I might have flirted back, but all I can manage now is a stilted chuckle.

"Hey, this guy bothering you?"

My heart leaps at the sound of the familiar voice. I almost jump to my feet and launch myself at Christian who's shooting Sawyer a very unimpressed look.

"What? You told me to keep Sebastian company."

"No, I asked you to tell him I'd be another couple minutes."

Sawyer stands to give Christian a smack on the shoulder. "Same thing. Anyway, great meeting you, Sebastian. I'll see you around." He waves and heads back to the front desk.

"Sorry about that. Sawyer is… Sawyer." Christian picks up the chair he just vacated and sets it next to mine before sitting down. "Hey, you all right?" Christian asks when I crowd into his personal space and press my face to his neck.

He smells a little musty and sweaty, but under that, he

smells like comfort, peacefulness, and home. The vise around my chest loosens enough for me to take a full breath. My heart stops trying to claw its way up my throat. I manage to unclench my hands and wrap them around one of Christian's instead.

"What happened? What's wrong?" Christian's voice is laced with worry and concern.

A part of my brain is telling me that everything's okay now that he's here, now that I'm in his arms. But another part is running around screaming that everything is wrong, that it's all about to come crumbling down around me, and I don't have enough hands to keep things in place.

"Sebastian, babe, breathe. Come on, breathe with me." He walks me through my breathing exercise, and with each cycle of inhales and exhales, my pulse slows a fraction or two.

"What's that exercise you told me about? The numbers one?"

"Five things I see?" I manage to squeak out.

"Yeah, that's it. What are five things you see?"

I force myself to open my eyes and list off the first five things they land on. Then four things I can feel—the heat of Christian's body, the callouses on his palms. Three things I can hear—Christian's deep, steady breathing, the rumble in his chest as he hums. Two things I can smell—the sweat on Christian's skin. And one thing I can taste—the lingering acidity from the mimosa at brunch.

The goddamn brunch.

"Good. Feel better?"

I nod, but I don't draw away from Christian.

"Do you need your medication?"

I shake my head. "I don't have it on me anyway."

"Do you want to go home to get it? I've got a break between clients. I can come with you."

I do want to go home. Not for my meds though. I want to drag Christian into bed with me and cuddle away the rest of the day. But he needs to work. And honestly, so do I.

"No, I'll be okay." For now, anyway. I might have narrowly avoided a full-blown anxiety attack, but the real problem is still looming over me like a thick, heavy cloud.

I sigh and force myself to pull away from Christian, just enough so I don't look like I'm trying to crawl into his lap, even though in his lap is where I want to be.

"So, uh, I was talking to the guys at brunch this morning." I stare at our clasped hands where Christian's thumb is brushing back and forth against my palm. Do I really want to bring this up? Maybe I should wait another week or so to see how things play out between us. I might be imagining our connection, or it'll start fading as the hype around us starts dying down.

"Yeah?"

I look up into Christian's eyes and let myself get caught up in them for a few seconds. I'm greedy for this feeling I get whenever I'm around him. That everything is going to be okay. That anything is possible. It makes me want to take the leap, to throw caution to the wind.

"They asked if we're going to do another video."

His thumb falters for a second, then picks back up. My stomach churns and my pulse stutters.

"What did you say?"

"That we hadn't talked about it." My voice is tight.

He nods but doesn't say anything. He looks surprised, but only like, a little. Like he was expecting this to come up at some point. And I suppose that makes sense. He is a professional. He'd know these things.

"They only asked because this one's doing so well, and normally I'd want to capitalize on the momentum and put another one out there quickly. But I know we only ever discussed one video, so I don't expect you to say yes. I mean, I don't even know if *I* want to. So yeah, never mind, sorry, forg—"

Christian's arm tightens around me and cuts short my rambling. "Hey, hey, slow down. Breathe."

I breathe. Once. Then again.

"Better?"

I nod. "Sorry."

"There's nothing to be sorry for," Christian says in that gruff voice of his that means I shouldn't try to argue with him. Christian extricates his hand from mine and cups my cheek. He swipes his thumb across it and stares into my eyes. His gaze is so strong, so intense, it sucks me in until I'm lost in it.

"You know, I'm not entirely opposed to the idea," Christian says with a quirk of his lips.

It takes a moment for his words to sink in. I blink when my brain manages to process them. "You're not?"

He shrugs. "Let's not rule it out just yet."

I open my mouth, then shut it again. I don't have any words to express how stunned I am. My heart is racing again but for an entirely different reason. My stomach settles itself back into my body and my lungs finally remember how to function. A part of me was convinced that Christian would never agree to another video. Or if he did, that would be the end of the relationship we're kinda, sorta building.

But here he is, considering the idea. And he's still holding me, caressing my cheek, smiling and looking at me in the way that I've become addicted to. Maybe there's a way to have both. Maybe it isn't too good to be true.

I move before I can talk myself out of it and surge toward him. I crush our mouths together and brace my hands on his cheeks to hold him close.

His arms come around me and suddenly I'm out of my chair and into his lap. I whimper against his lips and he opens his mouth for me. When our tongues touch, it sends a shudder of pleasure through me that pools in my groin. My cock fills and I can feel Christian's cock growing against my ass.

A catcall sounds somewhere off in the distance. It's Sawyer, I think, but it doesn't really matter. Christian's tongue is in my mouth and I'm keeping it there for as long as I can.

CHRISTIAN

"Are you sure about this?" Sebastian is surveying our hotel room in Chicago while twisting his fingers into knots.

I'm *not* sure about this at all. When this whole thing started, I only ever imagined myself doing one video. It was supposed to be a test, an experiment, just to see if I still had what it took. It's exploded into a completely different beast since then. I never expected the video to go viral like it has. I never expected to connect with Sebastian like we have either.

When he brought up the possibility of filming a second video, my first reaction was "No," followed immediately by "Why not?" I enjoyed it the first time. The video is doing really well. Sebastian's right that we should ride the wave as long as we can. The only factor that's firmly in the no column is the fact that I'm technically retired. And even that isn't quite as clear-cut as it used to be.

What I do know for sure is that I don't want to go back

to that old life of mine. I'm happy at Mars. I love being a personal trainer. I'm not about to give that up. But I like this too. I like the way Sebastian works—I like working *with* Sebastian. There's no reason why I can't have both in my life, is there?

I know Sebastian is apprehensive. I know he's got a lot more riding on these videos than I do. I also know that the prospect of not being successful, of not meeting his goals, is a constant worry that he carries around like a boulder on his back. If filming a second video will help alleviate that burden, then here, hold my jockstrap.

I take his hands and untangle his fingers. "I'm sure. Are *you* sure?"

He nods. His gaze flits to mine, then away. "Yeah, yeah, I'm sure."

He's a giant ball of energy, and has been since this morning when we were headed to the airport. I remember that mix of nervousness and excitement from our first shoot. He's fidgety and bouncing off the walls, eyes wide and a little wild. I draw him into my arms and after a second, he melts against me, letting me siphon away some of the excess restlessness.

Sebastian sighs. "Thank you."

I give him a squeeze. "That's what I'm here for."

He looks up at me with something in his eyes that I'm not sure I've seen before. Something a little hesitant and brimming with hope. It resonates with me, like some subconscious part of me recognizes it and reciprocates.

But before I can figure out what it is, or whether I should say something, Sebastian nods. "Okay, let's do this," he says, pulling away and turning to the suitcase with all his equipment.

It was my idea to film the follow-up video in Chicago. We've booked a fancy hotel room with black walls, plush leather furniture, and a giant king-sized bed covered in one-thousand thread count sheets. Out of the floor-to-ceiling windows is a view of Lake Michigan and the Centennial Ferris Wheel on Navy Pier. The art on the wall above the bed is some sort of spiky metal sculpture that looks kind of dangerous.

It'll be a change from Sebastian's apartment and we can tie it into the Grabby Awards. All points that should help hype up this sequel, which is what we're calling it. #*Chastian, the Sequel.*

We're starting in the bathroom, and it's a little tricky finding a spot for the tripod that gets the camera angles we want without drenching Sebastian's equipment. The shower is lined with dark, graphite tiles and fitted with a copper-colored rainwater shower head. It's deep and wide enough for two fully grown men, with a built-in bench that should garner some interesting positions.

Sebastian finishes fiddling with the camera and looks up at me. "That should do it." There's a tremor in his voice that gives away how amped up he is.

I go up to him, settle my hands on his hips, and pull him against me. "Hey."

His lips part as he sucks in a breath and I take the opportunity to slip my tongue into his mouth. He whimpers and clings to me, and blood rushes to my cock. Before the kiss in the lobby of Mars that day, we'd been astonishingly good at keeping our hands to ourselves. After that kiss though, all bets were off. I haul Sebastian into my lap every chance I get. I stop him in the middle of sentences to kiss him. It's like we're making up for all that lost time. And the more of Sebastian I get, the more I crave.

"Mmm," Sebastian moans into my mouth. "The camera's not on yet."

"I know. I'm just getting warmed up."

"Oh, okay." He gives me another kiss that I feel all the way down to my toes. "Warmed up?"

"Almost." I slide my hands down his back and fill my palms with his ass. I drag him against me so there's no doubt just how turned on I am by him. His own erection strains at his jeans and we grind against each other like this is the main event.

Sebastian breaks off the kiss. "How about now?"

I heave an exaggerated sigh. "Yeah, I guess so."

He gives me a little push. "You go first."

I step away from Sebastian and grab the hem of my t-shirt. I wait until I'm sure Sebastian is watching before slowly pulling it over my head, making sure to flex every muscle I can name as I go. Then my belt, which I pull out of the belt loops in one swift tug and drop to the tile floor with a clatter. I turn around for the next part, bending over as I push my jeans and underwear down my thighs.

There's a small crash behind me and when I look back, Sebastian is hastily trying to right a bunch of glass bottles on the counter.

"Sorry! Sorry!" He glances at me through the mirror and the bottles topple over again.

"Just leave them," I say, laughing.

Sebastian shoves them into the corner and carefully draws his hands back.

I step into the shower with a grin a mile wide. God,

he's so fucking adorable sometimes. I turn on the water and inch the handle around to find the right temperature. The thing with shower scenes is that they look hot on camera but they're a bitch to film. Can't crank it all the way to hot like a normal shower because the steam will fog up the camera lenses. Can't have it too cold or our balls will start retreating into our bodies. When I find something that's tolerable, I turn back to Sebastian. "Ready?"

He hits the record button on the camera. "Go ahead."

I step into the spray and tilt my head back to let the water run down my face, my chest, my thighs. I'm halfway to hard and a couple good strokes bring my cock to full attention.

"Fuck," Sebastian mutters, not so quietly from behind the camera. His hands are gripping the countertop so hard, his knuckles are white. And yet, he's leaning forward like a magnet drawn to its partner.

"Want to join me?" I've never seen anyone strip so fast. I smile as I turn toward the water and close my eyes to wait.

I feel the warmth of Sebastian's presence first and my skin tingles in anticipation. Even then, I jump when Sebastian's fingers land feather-light on my shoulders. I was expecting an attack, a full-on, body-on-body, frantic rutting together. But the gentle trail of Sebastian's touch down my back has me shuddering. My cock is rock hard.

I brace a hand on the wall in front of me and drop my chin to my chest as Sebastian caresses my back, my side, my hip, my ass. A groan rumbles out of me as he steps in closer and presses himself against me. His dick, already hard, slips in between my ass cheeks and the shiver that runs through me has nothing to do with the temperature of the water.

I turn and pull Sebastian to me, capturing his lips in a hard, deep kiss. Sebastian melts against me, clings to me, his fingers dig into my back like I'm the only thing keeping him upright. I fill my hands with him, stroke down his back, palm his ass. I hold him to me as I tilt my hips and rub my cock against his.

Jesus, he feels so good in my arms like this. All long, lean muscle, smooth and slick and perfect. I follow the trails of water flowing over his skin, licking down his neck and lapping at the dip above his collarbone.

Then down farther to a dusky nipple that I flick with my tongue. Sebastian gasps, so I do it again. I catch it between my teeth and give it a gentle tug, then rub my lips back and forth on it. Sebastian's breathing hard, he's making these shaky desperate sounds that bounce off the bathroom walls, he's got one hand on the back of my neck, gripping hard enough to leave marks.

The thought of it hits me low in the gut. I want him to leave marks on me. I want to leave marks on him. I want to see the evidence of our desire for each other and I want us to carry them on our bodies for days.

I latch onto random patches of skin, sucking them into my mouth until they're red and splotchy before making another. I work all the way down to his thighs, then sink my teeth into the meat of one of his quads. When Sebastian cries out, I soothe the bite with my tongue. Then I make a matching one on the other leg.

I'm down on my knees, Sebastian's long, thin cock bobbing right in front of me. I turn my face up, following the length of his body all the way to his eyes that are half-lidded with lust. He's panting through his mouth. The shower head is behind him and water cascades over his shoulders and down his front, a waterfall that I interrupt with my hands as I slide them over his body.

Sebastian is beyond gorgeous. His lips are rosy and bruised from our kisses. His skin is marred by my mouth, my teeth, my beard. His long, dark lashes are clumped together, but his eyes are just as hypnotizing as ever.

A wave of emotion crashes through me all of a sudden. It's so strong, so fast that I don't understand it, I can't tell one feeling apart from the next. They're all good feelings though. Happy ones, soft and tender ones. Ones that plunge deep into me and fill me up.

Sebastian draws his thumb across my brow, across my cheekbone, along my jaw, and through my beard. Does he see the emotions when he looks into my eyes? Does he see what he does to me? What he means to me? How we fit together like two halves of a whole?

He says that I was his inspiration, that I was the reason he started camming in the first place. Well, *he's* my inspiration, *he's* the reason why I came back to porn. I don't think I would've done it if it had been anyone else who'd approached me at Mars. No one has the allure he has. No one is as irresistible as he is.

I lock my gaze with his and lean forward to gently drag my beard across his hard, throbbing cock.

"Fuck!" His yell echoes and his grip tightens on the side of my face.

"Too much?"

"No, it's good. So fucking good."

I do it again along the other side. When the tip of his dick passes across my lips, I sneak my tongue out to snatch up the bead of pre-cum gathering there. Mmm, delicious. I wrap my lips around his cock, just the head, and suck.

"Oh god." Sebastian's body arches. His stomach muscles contract into a flat plane. His glutes clench in my palms.

I hum as more pre-cum lands on my tongue.

"Fuck, that feels good."

I'm about to make him feel even better. I slide my lips down his length, feeling every ridge and every bump along the way. He nudges the back of my throat and I swallow him down. He cries out but I keep going until my nose is pressed against his pelvis and his cock is lodged in my esophagus.

Sebastian's right. This does feel good. To have him fill my mouth and my throat. To taste him and smell him and touch him. To be surrounded by him. To be drowning in him. It feels right. It feels like I've been waiting for this my entire life.

CHAPTER
TWENTY-ONE

SEBASTIAN

Christian's mouth is heaven. On my dick, on my skin, on my own mouth—anytime it's on my body, I'm in heaven. And right now, it feels like I'm dying. He's got me lodged so far down his throat, I don't know if I'm going to get my cock back at all. At the rate he's sucking me, I'm going to blow my load before we even get out of the shower, then we won't have to bother with the second part of the video at all.

"Chris," I pant, just barely remembering to use his stage name. I push at his shoulders. "Too much. Oh god. Please."

He pulls off, only to replace his mouth with his hand, and smirks up at me. "Had enough?"

Yes. And no. I don't think I could ever get enough of him, of the way he looks at me with that laser-focus intensity, the way he calms me down with nothing but a simple touch. I run my palm over his short hair and his eyes flutter closed. He presses his face into my groin, takes a deep breath, and groans.

"Fuck, you always smell so good."

My cock jumps in his hand, at the way he's rubbing his face against my pelvis, his beard rough on my skin. At the way his groans rumble through me, hitting me in all the right places inside.

His other hand slides toward my crack and his fingers dip into the valley. He stills when he makes contact with the butt plug I'm wearing.

"Sebastian?" He glances up at me and I can't breathe when he looks at me like that. "What is this?"

He taps on the plug and it bumps against my prostate. I jolt, pushing my dick into Christian's fist. He taps on it again and I let out a high-pitched whimper. "Chris!"

He turns me around and presses against the back of one knee to get me to raise my leg. I plant my foot on the bench and bend forward to brace myself on the wall. Water hits the top of my head and runs down my back. Christian grabs both ass cheeks and pulls them apart.

"When did you put this in?" He traces a finger around the plug, then above and below, leaving a trail of fire in his wake.

"When I went to the bathroom after we landed." I wasn't about to go through security or sit on a plane with that thing inside me, but I remember how things went last time—I need as much prep as I can get.

Christian tightens his grip on my ass. "You mean you've been wearing the butt plug this whole time?" he growls.

I peer over my shoulder to find his eyes glued to the plug. He looks like he's about to dive in and devour it. My hole clenches involuntarily—I can't look at him when he's looking at me like that. I'll never last.

"Fuck." I turn to face forward again.

Christian wiggles the plug. "Going to take it out now," he warns.

I bear down as he tugs and it slides out of me with a pop.

"Fuck," Christian mutters behind me.

I'm loose and open. My hole is gaping and water flows over it, catches on it, leaks into me. Christian's finger is a hot poker and when he pushes inside, it feels like I'm being speared through.

I push back onto his hand. I need his fingers inside me. I want him to rip me open and stretch me wide. I crave the thickness of his cock, the length of it as it rearranges my insides to make space for itself. "Oh god, please."

Christian replaces his finger with his tongue and it's so much hotter than anything I've ever felt before. I'm being scalded, branded, marked as his.

He teases me, tongue darting in and out, swirling around in circles. His beard is rough as he rubs his chin up and down the valley of my crack, sending shivers of delight up my spine. My head spins and my cock throbs and there's so much pleasure surging through me, I can't hold still.

"Fuck, Chris." The words rip out of me in a desperate, needy sob.

Behind me, Christian growls again with his face buried right in there. The vibrations race through my hole and land deep in my groin. I could come like this. I *want* to come like this.

"Stop. Stop," I plead, trying to remember where we are and what we're supposed to be doing.

Christian relents. He gives me a sharp smack that sounds louder than it hurts and rakes his teeth across the swell of my ass. He kisses and sucks and rubs his way up my back until he catches my earring in his mouth. My cock jerks with every tug.

I writhe against him. Christian's cock slips into my crack and when he tilts his hips, the head catches against the rim of my hole. I need him in there. I need him filling me up.

"Okay, okay." Somehow, I find the strength to push him away. The second Christian releases me, I want to drag him back.

I collapse onto the bench in a tangle of limbs. I need to get up, turn the water off, move the equipment into the bedroom. If only my legs weren't jelly. If only there was enough oxygen in my brain for it to function.

Christian reaches past me and shuts the water off. He grabs a towel, unfurls it with a snap, and wraps it around me. He hauls me to my feet and I slump against him. He's so strong, so solid, and I feel so safe when I'm in his arms. I turn my head up and my gaze collides with his. His eyes are dark and heated. They burn me up from the inside out.

Then suddenly we're kissing, wet, hungry kisses that sound obscenely loud in the tiled bathroom. We stumble against a wall, my arms around his shoulders, his around my waist. We're clawing at each other, clinging to each other, like skin-to-skin isn't close enough, like we need to be inside each other.

Christian licks into my mouth, makes me suck on his tongue and swipes it over my palate and across my teeth until I'm whimpering. His hands are on my ass, gripping and kneading, and then he slides one even lower to prod at my hole from behind. My cock is pumping out a steady stream of pre-cum and it's so hard, it aches.

I'm not really even standing anymore. If it wasn't for Christian holding me up, I'd be a heap on the floor by now. When he finally releases my mouth, my head drops forward onto his shoulder as I struggle to sort out which way is up.

"Enough of the shower, I think," Christian mutters against my ear and I make a sound that I hope he interprets as agreement.

He pushes us away from the wall and I sway on my feet for a minute before I remember how feet are supposed to work. I feel all floaty, my entire body is tingly. All I can think about is getting Christian's cock inside me. Christian guides me out of the bathroom and to the bed. I'm sprawled on top of the covers before it occurs to me that I'm forgetting something.

"Wait, the cameras and stuff."

Christian plants a kiss on my head. "I'll get them."

I don't argue with him. I'll probably drop something if I tried to move stuff right now. It doesn't take him long to bring everything out and I let myself enjoy the view. His muscles bunch and flex as he moves. Those broad shoulders and thick thighs. His defined chest and the washboard stomach. His cock is huge and it bobs up and down as he walks. My mouth waters just looking at the thing. I want it down my throat.

"Is this okay?" Christian gestures to where he's placed the cameras.

I force myself off the bed and it feels like I'm moving

through molasses. Everything is slow and a little blurry. The air feels heavy and dense. I adjust the cameras as Christian rummages through his bag. He waits until I'm done before holding up his magic syringe. "Ready for this?"

My stomach clenches in want at the memory of the syringe all the way up inside me, at the feeling of being so thoroughly lubed.

I nod and slowly climb back onto the bed. Christian's hand is warm and firm on my hip. He rubs my lower back, my ass, my thigh, then reaches between my legs to fondle my raging hard cock. His thumb draws circles on my taint and his breath rushes hot over my skin. I sink into his touch, his sure, solid presence, and sigh.

"Ready?" Christian asks again. His voice is low and rumbly and it winds its way into me, filling me up.

"Mmhmm."

The tip of the syringe is cold and hard. I push out as Christian slides it in. It goes deep. So fucking deep. It doesn't hurt. It's just weird to have something touch me in there, something so unyielding. It only stays there for a second before Christian's pulling it out again, and in its wake is that squishy wetness of lube.

"All done." Christian presses a kiss to my tailbone, right at the top of my crack and the brush of his beard makes me shiver again.

I push myself to my knees and wiggle my hips back and forth.

"Does that feel okay?" Christian asks as he wraps up the syringe in a towel.

"Yeah. Just a little strange."

Christian glances toward me. His eyes are filled with

tenderness and affection and my heart fangirls a little—not because he's Chris Preacher, but because he's Christian. He's kind and caring. He's solid and steady. He keeps me grounded. He keeps me and my dysfunctional brain from spiraling out of control.

He comes to me and wraps his hand around the back of my neck. This kiss is soft and gentle. I mold myself to him and our erections bump together, reminding me of the idea I had earlier.

"I want to deep-throat you," I murmur against Christian's lips.

He stills and when he pulls away to look at me, the heat in his eyes is scorching. "Yeah?"

I nod. "I can lie on the bed. I think it should be the right height."

Christian swallows and I lean in for an open-mouthed kiss on his neck, right where his pulse beats. It's fast and strong and mine hurries to match it.

"Okay."

I'm just coherent enough to make sure all the cameras are properly positioned, in focus, and recording, then I spot my phone sitting on the nightstand. I hold it up. "Film it?"

Christian takes it from me. "Get up there."

I've done this a couple times before, but never with someone as big as Christian. A shudder runs through me when I'm on my back, head hanging over the edge of the bed, eye to eye with his monster. He's going to choke me with that thing, he's going to suffocate me—and I can't wait.

Christian's holding the phone in one hand and his cock in the other. He rubs the tip across my lips, smearing them with his salty, bitter pre-cum. I lick it up and chase his cock for more. When I wrap my lips around the crown and suck, I'm rewarded with a nice, thick gush. Christian groans.

I reach for the backs of his thighs to pull him closer. He feeds his cock to me, inch after inch. He hits the back of my throat and it still feels like there's so much more. I breathe in, using every yoga breathing trick I know to fill my lungs, then I tug him closer still. With a swallow, he slides into my throat.

"Fuck." Christian's thighs quiver under my hands. His balls are resting on my face. I'm smothered in his crotch and this might be my favorite place in the entire world.

"I can see it," Christian whispers with reverence in his voice. He touches my throat where I'm sure it's bulging out. He's gentle and I swallow again. "Oh my god, that feels so good. Fuck, Sebastian." He tries to pull back, but I keep him there. I can hang on for a few extra seconds.

He sounds strained, desperate, coming apart. I hum, knowing I'm the one doing this to him. *I'm* the one making him tremble.

"Fuck." Christian tries to pull back again and this time I let him.

"Fuck my throat," I say before swallowing him down again.

"Jesus Christ—are you sure?"

I can feel the tension in Christian's legs as he struggles to hold himself still. I moan around him and tighten my grip on his thighs to encourage him. He lets out a litany of curses and starts moving his hips. Slowly. So slowly. Like he's worshiping my throat with his cock rather than fucking it.

I let him set the pace and the depth. I trust Christian. He's not going to risk hurting me. I relax my fingers, my jaw, my throat. He slips his hand behind my neck to support me.

Christian speeds up, slipping deep into my throat, then pulling out far enough so I can catch my next breath. His balls slap me in the face with weighty *thwacks*. My saliva leaks out of the corner of my mouth and down my cheeks. My eyes are shut and I fall into that place of semi-consciousness where it's all pleasant sensations all the time.

I don't know how long we do this for. I don't really care. I could lie there all day letting Christian use my throat if he wanted to. I don't need to breathe. I don't need water or food. All I need is Christian inside me, making me whole.

CHAPTER
TWENTY-TWO

CHRISTIAN

Sebastian is amazing. Well no, he's more than amazing, but I don't have the vocabulary to describe just how wonderfully, astonishingly mind-blowing he is.

I don't know if he's going to be able to use anything I've filmed on his phone. I'm shaking too hard. I can't keep my hand steady. I'm more concerned about not hurting Sebastian than about keeping the camera pointed in the right direction.

I want to come down his throat. I want to fill his stomach with my cum. I want him to taste me on his tongue for days.

I carefully ease my way out of his mouth. Any more and I'll really lose it.

My cock is soaked in Sebastian's spit and long strands connect me back to his mouth. His face is wet with it. I bend down to smash my mouth against his, lick up all that saliva, and push it back between his lips.

Sebastian's whimpers are lower than they normally

are. His throat has to be raw from my fucking. His fingers dig into my shoulders, the back of my neck and my head, like he can't get enough of me, like he wants more.

I want more too. I haven't gotten nearly enough of him. I'm not sure I ever will.

I haul Sebastian upright and rearrange him on the bed so we're angled properly with the cameras. I settle next to him, my weight causing the mattress to sink, and Sebastian slides in a little closer. My head's propped up on my arm as I gaze down at Sebastian.

He's floating somewhere in semi-consciousness, eyes barely open, unfocused. His lips are red and swollen. The rest of his face is splotchy. He's already covered in a sheen of sweat that glistens off his olive-tan skin. His dick is so engorged, the head is purple and the veins look like they might burst.

He turns into me like he can't stand to have anything between us. I know how he feels. "Hold on. We'll get there."

He whimpers.

I hook my foot around Sebastian's knee and pull it toward me, then I push the other knee away to spread his thighs. I run my hand up his inner thigh, fondle his heavy balls, then slide my fingers over his taint to his hole. There's a lot of lube leaking out of him already and I smear my fingers through it.

"I'm prepped," Sebastian complains as he tries to tug me on top of him.

"I know," I grin and give him a quick kiss. "But I've been dreaming of this." I sink a finger into his body and Sebastian gasps.

The look on Sebastian's face is pure lust and it makes

my cock jump. I insert a second finger and Sebastian shudders. His hole flutters around my hand and when I brush against his prostate, he lets out a beautiful cry.

I kiss him. He's too delicious not to kiss. I push my tongue into his mouth just as I push my fingers into his ass.

This isn't just sex between industry colleagues, or even between friends. The realization crashes through me, shattering everything I assumed I knew about what was going on here. I have feelings for Sebastian—strong feelings, ones that threaten to overwhelm me. I want to give him everything. I want to be his everything. I want him to come apart in my arms and then I want to slowly piece him back together.

"Sebastian," I whisper, my voice tight with all the emotion coursing through me. "Look at me."

"Hmm." He blinks but doesn't see anything.

"Please, babe, look at me."

His eyes flutter open and it takes a minute for his pupils to focus enough to see me. His eyes are golden brown, shiny with the light reflecting off them. They're the prettiest eyes I've ever seen.

Sebastian's expression changes as he gazes up at me. He can probably read everything I'm feeling right there on my face. His eyes fill with tears that spill out of the corners onto his temples. I kiss them up.

He cups my face with his hands. "Christian," he whispers and I hear it in his voice, all the things he feels for me too.

That's all I can take. I unceremoniously tear my finger out of Sebastian's ass and shift to settle my hips between his thighs. I don't want to hurt him, but I can't wait any longer. I notch the head of my cock against his hole and press, slow and unrelenting, inch by inch, sinking into his heat.

Sebastian's lust-filled eyes snap into sharp focus and he stares squarely at me. I stare right back. Something's happening here, something more than sex, more than the connection we felt last time. This is deeper, more profound, more elemental.

Irreversible.

I don't know how we managed to get this far without realizing what was happening. Even if we pulled back now, even if we stopped filming right this second and never saw each other again, I don't think it would make a difference. We've both been changed so fundamentally there's no going back. We need each other, desperately, helplessly, hopelessly.

I bottom out and Sebastian sucks in a hiss. I catch the tail end of it, eating it up with my tongue in his mouth. This mouth that I fucked mere minutes ago. That had cradled my cock so perfectly. This magnificent, mind-blowing mouth.

Sebastian wraps his legs around my waist and his arms around my neck. I fall hard—into his body, my dick consumed, my weight pinning him to the mattress. And a part of my soul falls into Sebastian's too. We're being bound together, twisted and tight. Every second we spend in each other's arms weaves us closer and closer until we become one. I slip my arms under Sebastian and bury my face into the crook of his neck, breathing in his teasingly vanilla scent, mixed with our sweat and our sex.

"Christian." He breathes in my ear.

That's all the encouragement I need. I fuck him, slow

then fast, shallow then deep. My body responds to Sebastian's like it's never responded to anyone before. We move in sync, pulling apart only to slam back together again. Sebastian's cries ring out over my own grunts and groans.

"I'm going to come. Oh fuck, I'm going to come," Sebastian yells, his body shaking uncontrollably.

I try to sit up so the camera can capture the cum shot, but Sebastian tightens his hold. His fingers dig into my back, his ankles lock around my waist. Yes, that's where I want to be too.

I cradle Sebastian's ass in my palm, holding him close to make sure my dick presses against his prostate. His cock rubs slick and wet against my stomach.

Sebastian cries out again, tossing his head back, arching off the bed. Hot cum spurts between us, again and again, as every muscle in Sebastian's body goes taut.

There's no way I could've held it off. Not with how tightly Sebastian's clamping down on my cock. Not with Sebastian's arms and legs still locked behind me. I have no choice but to thrust as deep into Sebastian as I can and surrender to the orgasm racing through me.

A roar fills my ears. White spots dance on the back of my eyelids. I'm torn, limb from limb, until I'm nothing more than a sack of flesh slumped against Sebastian. And even then, he doesn't let me go.

A seed of truth threads through the aftershocks of my orgasm and implants itself deep inside me. Whatever happens after all this, I'll be his forever.

CHAPTER
TWENTY-THREE

SEBASTIAN

Reality comes back to me slowly. Or maybe I'm the one coming back to reality. Either way, Christian and I lie there for a long time, all wrapped up in each other. He slips out of me, leaving me open, wet, and empty. My cum is drying between our bodies. When I finally open my eyes, Christian is watching me.

"Hey," he says, his voice thick with emotion.

"Hey," I whisper back.

I feel different. Like I'm not quite myself. It feels like the ground has shifted under my feet and what I thought was up isn't up anymore. I'm strangely okay with it, with this new orientation of my world. The fact that I'm okay with it, though, that's what kind of freaks me out.

Something happened between us during that scene. Can we even call it a scene? I forgot about the cameras the second I climbed onto the bed. I forgot about angles and framing and making sure there'd be enough footage for a full-length video. It was all Christian—his mouth, his hands, his cock. Him above me, around me, and inside of me. He filled me up in all the ways I can be filled and now my heart is overflowing with him.

Christian rolls off to the side and I reluctantly let him go. I shiver—from the rush of cold air over my skin, but also because I'm kind of in shock. The intensity of what we did is wearing off now, leaving me weak and shaken and off-kilter. My head spins when I sit up, my stomach feels like I've just stepped off a rollercoaster. I move slowly as I check the cameras and shut them down.

Then Christian puts his arm around my waist and takes me back to the shower. He cranks the water all the way to hot this time and steam quickly fills the room. We don't speak as he rubs soap into my skin.

My head falls back onto his shoulder and he presses a kiss to my neck as his hands roam my front.

"Sorry," he murmurs.

"For what?"

"This doesn't smell like vanilla."

It takes several moments for me to figure out what he's talking about. "Oh, my body wash?"

"Hmm." He's gentle as he soaps around my cock, my balls, and back to my taint. "I love the way you smell. Like chocolate chip cookies."

I laugh and it almost sounds hysterical with glee.

He sets me away from him to soap my back. When he gets down to my ass, he takes his time pulling my cheeks apart and covering every inch of my crack, dipping into my loose hole. I push out for him and he growls before sinking his teeth into the fleshy part of my butt.

I'm covered in Christian's marks. Hickeys and beard burn dot the front of my body. I can only imagine what my back looks like. I trace them, lingering on each one before moving to the next. It makes me giggle, seeing the evidence of Christian on my body. It feels kinda like he's marking his territory, and I'm undoubtedly his.

Pure delight wells up in me, threatening to overwhelm me. Who would have ever guessed that my teenage idol would turn out to be so kind and caring and supportive? Who would have ever thought that my teenage fantasies would one day come true?

Christian finishes with my legs and I turn into his arms.

"Hey," I say.

His eyes are dark and his hands grip me tight. "Hey."

I kiss him, a hard press of my lips to his. Holy hell—I love him. If this burst of happiness, this explosion of joy isn't love, then I don't know what is. I love him so much, it hurts. It feels like my heart is trying to claw its way out of my body so it can go live inside his. Like my lungs would rather feed him oxygen than save any for myself.

Christian takes one of his deep breaths that expands his chest and makes me all swoony. I try to breathe too, to create some more space inside me, but every inch I stretch gets filled with love for him, leaving me stuffed and brimming.

I take the soap from Christian and he stands still as I return the favor of soaping him up. The round bulges of his biceps, the smooth curves of his chest. The hills and valleys of his abs. His thighs are thick and ropy with muscle. His calves fill my entire hand.

His ass is a masterpiece—round and hard, with matching dips on either side. The small of his back is a perfectly narrow slope. His back—Christ, his back. There are no words for how gorgeous those miles of skin are.

I draw my fingers down each of his arms, following the lines of his tattoos. And when I'm done, he takes my hands and weaves our fingers together so we're palm to palm.

Christian might never feel the same way about me, he might never be able to return my love. But that's okay. It almost feels like too much to ask, really. He's already here, working with me, spending time with me. If friendship is all I ever get, then I'll satisfy myself with that.

We order room service for dinner and eat it on the couch wearing nothing but our underwear. The lights of the city blink below us and the sound of the TV is turned down low.

We don't talk much. There's no need to. We've spent weeks and weeks talking and now we can sit and soak in each other's presence. It's lovely. It feels like we're in a bubble, separated from the world. Everyone else might rush on with their lives, but here, time is on pause.

We eventually turn the TV and the lights off and climb into bed. I'm cuddled up in Christian's arms, head on his shoulder. This is it. This is where I'm happy. This is where I belong. I can't think of anything better.

When I wake up in the morning, I'm alone in bed. I bury my face into Christian's pillow—it's cold, but it still smells like him.

"Christian?" I call out, but the room is too silent for him to be hiding somewhere. Just then, the door's lock beeps and it swings open.

Christian appears looking sinful in those joggers I love and a very form-fitting t-shirt.

"Hey, good morning."

"Mmm." I stretch and the covers slide down to uncover my chest, my stomach, and a bit of my hip.

Christian sets what I think is breakfast down on the coffee table by the couch, then comes to sit next to me. He places his hand at the base of my neck and drags it down my body, pausing to flick a nipple, then trace my belly button. He pushes the covers down to my knees and slides his hand between them to run his palm up my inner thigh.

My breath hitches as he gets closer and closer to my aching cock, but rather than wrap his hand around it, he hooks his thumb into the crease of my hip and presses his fingers behind my balls. He caresses my taint and brushes lightly against my hole.

Fuck, I want him again. I want his mouth on me, his fingers in me. I want all of Christian, all the time.

"How do you feel?" Christian asks, voice husky.

"Good." I tilt my hips forward. "I could be better?"

"Yeah?"

"Mmm." I peer up at him and curl my lips into a smile.

His eyes heat as his hand tightens on me and a low growl comes from deep within him. He bends down to kiss me, despite my morning breath, then makes his way across my body to touch up the marks he left on me yesterday.

When he gets to my cock, he licks a wide stripe from the base to the tip. He wraps his lips around me and takes me in to the hilt.

"Christian!" I grab his shoulder, the back of his head. More for something to hang on to than to direct his movements. He doesn't need me to tell him what to do—Christian's a fucking maestro at blowjobs.

And fuck, does he suck. His cheeks hollow out as he drags his lips along my length. His tongue digs into my slit and pleasure shoots down to my balls. With one hand, he fondles my balls and with the other, he twists my nipples between his fingers. I whimper and writhe under him as he plays my body like we've been together for ages.

He's going at me so hard and fast my orgasm comes rushing at me. I barely have time to warn him before my cock explodes and I empty my balls into his mouth. Christian wraps a hand around my length and pumps every last drop out onto his tongue. Then he takes my chin, opens my mouth, and feeds my cum back to me.

Fuck, that's dirty. My dick twitches at how much I love it. At how much I love everything Christian does to me. And how much I love him.

"Is that better?" Christian murmurs against my lips.

I nod. "Much." Then I reach for him. He's hard under the soft fabric of his joggers. I want that thing in my mouth. I want it choking me. I want to swallow down his cum too so we're all mixed together in my stomach.

But Christian gently pries my hand away. "Later."

I pout. "Promise?"

"Promise."

After breakfast, Christian makes us visit the fitness room at the hotel. I'd rather go for a run, but I figure I can get more pictures of us this way.

I take one of him on the bench press, lying on his back while I'm looking down at him from above. My legs and shoes are in the shot and it almost looks like I'm about to straddle his face.

Then one in the mirror while he's doing biceps curls and I'm draped all over him. Then a selfie when Christian's on the leg press and I squeeze myself in next to him so it looks like we're lying down together.

Okay, so Christian works out and I just take a bunch of photos for social media. He doesn't seem to mind though, if his casual touches, full-body hugs, and bright smile are any indication.

I post a few of the photos online while we're on the way up to our room for a shower and the likes and comments immediately start pouring in.

"Whoa," he whispers, peering over my shoulder. I lean back against him and tug his arms tighter around my waist.

"Yup."

"Is it like that every time?"

"Every time."

"Can't you turn off the notifications?"

I sigh and slip my phone into my pocket. "I can and I do sometimes. But I try to respond to some of the comments and engage with the fans, so I don't really mind the notifications."

I tuck myself under his arm as we stroll from the elevator to our room.

"So you're basically working twenty-four-seven," Christian says. He holds the door open for me.

"Seven days a week, three-sixty-five."

He frowns as he peels his shirt off and steps out of his shorts. I don't really need a shower—hard to work up a sweat when all I've done is take pictures. But I strip alongside him and let him drag me into the shower.

I'm determined to get my mouth on his cock this time. I push him down onto the bench and settle myself on my knees between his legs. He's built like a freaking god—all those muscles, plump and perfectly sized for my hands. I run my palms up his thighs, over his stomach, and up to his chest. It still feels like a dream sometimes, like this can't possibly be real.

His cock is semi-hard when I take it into my mouth. I drag my tongue over it and shiver as it grows and hardens. A surge of power rushes through me knowing that I have this kind of effect on Christian. I can make him aroused. I can make him lose control.

I drag my lips over the thick vein running along the underside of his dick. I flick my tongue against that little dip underneath the head. I lap up his pre-cum, wiggling my tongue into his slit for more.

I stuff his cock as far into my throat as it'll go. My jaw is fully extended, my tongue is flat against his length, and I choke myself on the bulb of his head. I can't get it all the way in like when I was on the bed with my head tilted back, but I manage some of it. When I swallow around his head, he grunts, and his body jerks.

"Sebastian," he growls and that spurs me on.

I lose myself on Christian's cock. I blow him until my jaw is sore, until my throat is raw, until the tiles on the shower floor dig painfully into my knees. I suck on his cock like it's my singular mission in life, like his cum is the elixir I need to live. I take more and more of him until I'm mindless, high on his flesh in my mouth, his hands in my hair, his smell in my nose.

Then I do it. I swallow and suddenly I'm nose to pelvis. I can't breathe, I can't move, I've impaled myself on Christian's cock. If I die here, it will be a good death.

"Fuck, fuck, Sebastian." Christian's shaking as he tries to hold still for me. He cups my cheek, then slides his hand down to feel his own dick lodged halfway in my neck. "Fuck, I'm going to come."

I hum. I want him to come like this. Directly down my throat so I can't even taste him. Just pump all his thick ropy cum straight into my stomach.

His dick swells impossibly large in my mouth. I think my esophagus is going to rupture with how thick he is. I'm almost certainly going to pass out. But I can feel every pulse of pleasure that crashes through him, I can feel his cock jerking and twitching inside me.

I cough when Christian eases himself out of me. I'm barely conscious when he hauls me up into his lap and tucks my head under his chin. He kisses me on the forehead and I nuzzle my nose against his neck as I float away.

CHAPTER
TWENTY-FOUR

CHRISTIAN

Sebastian's armed with the camera on his phone when we step outside to wander the city. The sun feels brighter, the air smells a little sweeter, and I can't seem to wipe this silly grin off my face. Sebastian seems just as happy and bubbly as I am, and every time he directs his smile at me, it hits me like a blast cannon. I feel like a teenager, discovering the giddy high of romance for the first time.

Last night and this morning were so simple, so effortless. Everything from getting ready for bed to where we're spending our day to what kind of food to get for lunch… it's comfortable, uncomplicated, and soothing. We fit together seamlessly, like we were custom created for each other. I can't remember what my life was like before Sebastian barged into it. I can't imagine ever having lived without him. I reach for him whenever my hands are free. I feel an ache in my chest if I haven't heard his voice in too long. I've never craved chocolate chip cookies so damn much.

We head back to the hotel late in the afternoon to get ready for the awards show. The dress code for the Grabby's is literally whatever people want to wear—or not wear, as the case may be. There are as many practically naked attendees as there are those dressed in tuxes and every conceivable style in between.

I've got on a black-on-black three-piece suit, with a black shirt and a black tie. It's highlighted with satin lapels and a silver watch chain clipped to my vest. I bought the outfit especially for this occasion, wanting to look my best as I walk down the red carpet next to Sebastian. I want to make him look good.

I'm combing out my beard when Sebastian comes out of the bathroom.

"What do you think?" He holds out his arms.

He's wearing a dark blue suit with a crisp white shirt, open at the collar, and a bright pink handkerchief in his breast pocket. It reeks of a casual elegance that not many guys can pull off. Sebastian does, though, like this is the type of stuff he wears every day. His hair is artfully styled and I think he's got some makeup on under his eyes.

He swallows and my gaze is drawn to the base of his neck, that delicate little dip there that's calling my name. I take a step toward him, wanting to seal my lips around his skin and suck until I leave a mark. I don't though—there's already a hickey on his chest that's barely covered by his open collar.

"You look amazing." I draw him to me.

He winds his arms underneath my suit jacket and around my waist, and there's something so intimate about that that my heart swells until it feels like it's going to burst out of my chest.

"You look pretty good too."

"Only pretty good?"

"I mean, I prefer you naked, but this will do."

I growl and catch his lips in a kiss. He melts into me and I'm sorely tempted to skip the whole show and stay in. If only Sebastian wasn't up for an award.

The car we reserved is waiting for us when we get down to the lobby. I wave the driver away and open the door for Sebastian. He smiles up at me through his lashes and I have to actively tamp down my lust. I climb in after him and drag him across the seat so he's sitting plastered to my side. That's as far as I'm willing to let him go tonight.

The drive is short and before I know it, we're thrown into the organized chaos of a red carpet. It's been ages since I've been to one of these things and I immediately remember why I don't miss it one bit.

It's loud as photographers shout for our attention and interviewers yell questions in our faces. Event organizers shove us along what feels like a meat processing line. I never know where to look or who is trying to talk to me. The massive floodlights have me sweating under my collar already. Maybe the guys who opt out of clothing have the right idea.

"You okay?" Sebastian asks as we pause between two pre-marked spots where we're waiting to pose in front of a bank of photographers.

I take a deep breath and tug Sebastian closer. "Yeah, it's just been a while."

"You're doing great. All you have to do is relax and smile." He reaches up to adjust my tie and pick off a piece of lint.

If Sebastian is sweating under these lights, I can't tell. In fact, he doesn't seem nervous or uncomfortable at all. He looks like he was born to walk the red carpet, soak up the attention, and shine it back in a dazzling display of brilliance and charm. Sebastian is made for this world. He thrives in it.

Me? If I had any doubts coming into this evening, the last ten minutes have confirmed that this type of mayhem isn't the life for me anymore.

"Sebastian Silver!"

"Chris Preacher!"

Our names barely register in my mind before Sebastian slips his hand into mine and pulls me into the spotlight. When we hit our mark, I wrap my arm around Sebastian's waist and he leans back against me. I can smell the scent of our hotel soap mixed with Sebastian's signature vanilla.

The fans and the media have all speculated on our official relationship status and the pictures Sebastian's posted of us have done nothing to dissuade them. In my mind— in my heart—I know we're more than mere colleagues or even friends. We're something to each other, even if we haven't defined what that is.

Standing here in front of all the cameras, though, seeing how *on* Sebastian is, I'm struck by a moment of uncertainty. What if we're letting all this attention muddle what's really going on between us? Yeah, sure, we have explosive sex. And yeah, all of our "dates" have been a lot of fun. We can talk about anything and we can sit with each other in silence. But everything we've done so far has been in front of a camera, carefully documented for public consumption… for public validation.

I'm probably overthinking things and letting the big

flashing lights get to me. And yet, as we smile for the photographers and answer questions from interviewers, I can't get that thought out of my head. What if we've convinced ourselves this is real, but it isn't? What if this relationship can only exist in the public eye?

"Chris, Sebastian—let's put the rumors to rest once and for all. Are you two an item?" An interviewer sticks a microphone in Sebastian's face. This is the third time someone's asked us this question as we work our way down the line.

Sebastian's been doing all the talking on the red carpet and I'm in no hurry to replace him. He laughs and turns to me. He puts his hand on my chest and I stare down into his eyes.

"We're just really good friends," he says into the microphone, knowing full well he's not putting any rumors to rest with that answer.

"Friends with explosive chemistry! Tell me, are we going to get a sequel to that smoking-hot video of you guys?"

Sebastian shrugs and smiles mischievously. "You'll have to wait and see!"

The interviewer turns to me. "Chris, what's it like getting back in the game? Especially with Sebastian?"

I know what I'm supposed to say. It's what everyone expects of me. Even then, I glance at Sebastian and let my gaze linger for a moment, taking in how his eyes are shining, how he's radiating with energy. Then I turn back to the interviewer who has obviously watched every second of that subtle interaction.

"It's great," I say and then smile like I've got a secret that I'm not going to tell. Guess I'm not above fueling the rumors myself, but that's the game, right? Drum up interest in whatever way we can.

A beat passes before the interviewer realizes that's all they're getting from me. "Short and to the point. I like it! Well, it's safe to say that fans cannot get enough of the two of you, so we hope we'll be getting more soon. Enjoy the evening!"

I keep my hand on Sebastian's lower back as we move on. More questions about our relationship. More questions about whether there will be another video. More questions about what it's like being back, or whether I've got more projects in the works. By the time we reach the end of the red carpet and get ushered into the ballroom, I'm exhausted and ready to get out of here.

"Hey, you were great." Sebastian smooths his palms over my lapels.

I sneak my hands under the hem of his suit jacket to settle them over his hips. "*You* were great. I was just arm candy."

"Sebby!"

Sebastian turns and breaks out into a smile. "Hey!"

Three guys approach us. I've seen one of them before… in one of Sebastian's videos. He's tall and slim with dark hair and dark eyes. Noel, I think his name is.

The one who came running up to Sebastian is shorter, petite with dark makeup around his eyes. He pulls Sebastian into a hug and rocks them side to side. The last guy is quieter, blond with striking green eyes, and he hangs half a step back with a small smile on his lips.

"Christian, let me introduce you to my friends." Sebastian points to each one. "Noel, Rhys, and Hayden. Guys, this is Chris Preacher!"

These are the guys he goes to brunch with, the ones he's discussed me with, and they crowd around me like they're comparing me to what Sebastian's told them.

"Hello, so nice to finally see you." Rhys gives me the once-over. "You're taller in person."

Sebastian coughs and I have to wonder whether "tall" is a euphemism for something else.

"Hi, great meeting you." Hayden shakes my hand with a firm grip, then steps back again.

It's Noel who's studying me with a shrewd look. He doesn't seem like a guy who misses anything. I give him a nod and he gives me a nod back.

"We're all over here!" Rhys waves for us to follow him.

Noel falls into step next to me. "So, you and Sebastian, huh?"

I shoot him a look out of the corner of my eyes. "Yeah."

"I've never seen him like this before."

"Oh? Like what?"

"Having so much fun."

I don't know what I'd expected Noel to say, but it certainly wasn't that. What does it even mean?

Noel slows to a stop and I stop with him. His voice is low when he speaks. "Sebastian tends to get himself wound up a lot. But since you two started hanging out, he's been a lot more relaxed." Noel stares me in the eyes. "It's good for him."

I stare back. He thinks I'm good for Sebastian. The thought makes my chest puff up and my heart does a few somersaults in a row.

Noel and I share a moment of understanding before he turns to head toward our table. He stops and leans in toward me. "By the way, it wasn't because of a limp dick, was it?"

I reel back. "What?"

He shakes his head and waves his hand. "Never mind. I'm sure it was nothing." Then he leaves me to take his seat next to Rhys and Hayden.

"What was that about?" Sebastian asks when I sit down next to him.

"Something about a limp dick?"

He groans and buries his face in his hands. "Oh my god."

"Do you know what it means?"

He shoots Noel a dirty look and Noel smirks. "Yeah, I'll tell you about it later."

CHAPTER
TWENTY-FIVE

SEBASTIAN

I am going to kill Noel. I *cannot* believe he said that to Christian! I'd march around the table and strangle him if the show wasn't about to start and if there weren't half a dozen cameras watching our every move.

The lights in the ballroom dim and the host for the evening launches into his opening monologue. It's funny, I think, since everyone's laughing. I don't really hear much of it.

Christian has angled his chair so he's a little bit behind mine and it feels like he's sitting around me rather than merely next to me. His arm is draped across the back of my seat and his hand rubs absently up and down my arm. It's casual and familiar, exactly the kind of vibe we want to exude. Except I'd rather be in his lap, head on his shoulder, his arms all the way around me.

I need his touch. I need the way he grounds me. Because my anxiety is creeping in around the edges of my mind—slowly, but steadily.

It started as we were getting ready for the show. I thought it was a normal case of nervousness and excitement. Getting all dressed up, anticipating the lights and cameras, rubbing elbows with the most influential people in the industry. The possibility of winning an award that would be a huge freaking validation of the hard work I've put in over the years. Of course I'd be fidgety and jumpy. Of course my skin would be tingly and my tummy fluttery. It hadn't occurred to me that it could be anything more serious until we stepped out of the car and onto the red carpet.

Then the bubbly, ticklish feeling started edging into jittery and antsy and it's only gotten worse since. It's like something inky dark and suffocating is snapping at my heels, trying to crawl up my back. It's got my stomach all tied up in knots and my lungs paralyzed and my heart bouncing around in my chest.

I wish I'd taken my medication before leaving the hotel. I wish I'd brought some of it with me. I wish I hadn't been so freaking distracted by the bright and shiny that I completely missed the warning signs along the way. But it's too late. I don't have my medication on me. And even if I popped a pill now it would take at least an hour before it'd have any effect. I'll just have to steel myself and push through it.

I think I managed okay in front of all those cameras on the red carpet—the result of years of learning how to shut myself down, plaster a smile on my face, and push through whatever chaos is raging in my mind. It only means I'll crash harder afterward, but hopefully, that won't be until after the show.

I would be so much worse if Christian wasn't right

beside me, hand on my back, on my waist, body pressed right up against mine. He's my single tether to reality, the anchor that's keeping my mind from spiraling. The gentle caress of his hand on my arm, the brush of his lips against my ear when he leans in to whisper something, the thickness of his thigh under my palm—I focus on those things rather than the large stage and the bright lights and the camera guys crouching right in front of me, zooming in for a close up of my face.

I've done such a good job of ignoring the show that I'm startled when my category is suddenly up next. I scramble for Christian's hand and when he grips mine, I feel a tad less like throwing up.

"You've got this," Christian murmurs in my ear as a camera guy zooms in, broadcasting our image on the ginormous screen on stage.

The presenter is the guy who beat me in this category last year and despite all that talk about it being an honor just to be nominated, I've harbored a tiny bit of resentment toward him ever since. It's nothing personal—I wanted to win.

I want to win this year too. Of course I do. I've met or know of all the guys I'm up against. They're good at what they do and I can see why each of them have been nominated. I can also see why each of them has a better chance of winning than I do.

The presenter reads each of our names. My pulse is racing and I'm gripping Christian's hand so tightly, I'm sure I'm leaving bruises. The smile I've plastered on my face all night feels like a plastic mask. I only manage tiny little breaths as the guy on stage opens the envelope and pauses for dramatic effect.

"And the award for Most Sex-Positive Performer goes to... Sebastian Silver!"

Chaos erupts all around me and I'm hauled to my feet. I'm not entirely sure what's going on until Christian holds my face with both hands and stares into my eyes.

"You did it! You won!" He plants a big, non-apologetic kiss on my lips and I'm too stunned to do anything but stand there like a mannequin.

I won? Holy shit, I won.

I don't know how I manage to get up on the stage. Words come spilling out of my mouth—something about gratitude and loving ourselves and accepting others. The audience chuckles, so maybe I've thrown a joke in there. The specifics are hazy. The only clear thing in my mind is the weight of the statue that I clutch to my chest like it's some sort of life preserver.

The awards show people usher me off the stage and through an obstacle course of photographers and inter-viewers. Who the hell knows what I look like or what I say. If I'm a deer in headlights and am completely incoherent, maybe they'll chalk it up to the whirlwind of the win rather than my brain freaking out on me.

I don't really come back to myself until I'm spat back out into the ballroom. The show is still going strong, the host is telling some joke that has the audience howling. I pick my way through the tables back to Christian and gently lower myself into my chair.

"Where's your award?" Christian asks.

"Huh?" I stare at my hands. Where *is* the award? I have a vague memory of people taking it from me at some point. "I think that was just a prop. They said something about sending me the real thing after."

"Are you okay?" Christian tugs me around to face him.

"Huh?"

"Sebastian?"

I look up at him and the mask I've been working so hard to maintain all evening crumbles. Christian's eyes grow wide and he mutters a curse under his breath.

"Come on, let's go." He takes my hand and tries to stand, but I drag him back down.

"Go where?"

"Out, back to our hotel, anywhere."

I shake my head. "But the show's not over yet."

"Who cares about the show? The important part's over anyway."

I shake my head. No, I can't leave. Not in front of everyone like this. Not when everyone will see and wonder and ask questions.

Christian lets out a low growl, then grabs me around the waist and hauls me into his lap. He tucks me in close and secures his arms around me. I melt into him, into his warmth, his strength, his steadiness. It's better than my medication, better than exercise, better than any other distraction I've ever been able to find. He yanks my mind back into the present and keeps it there, safe and secure.

"Five things," he mutters into my ear.

My gaze darts around us to see who's watching—most of our table and a few others at the table next to us. Do they know? Can they tell? Or will they assume this is us being clingy?

Christian shoves his hand in between mine to give me something to grab on to. "Five things," he growls again.

Okay, fine. I force myself to run through the list and whisper it to him. My lips brush against the shell of his ear and I hope that anyone watching will think I'm murmuring sweet nothings. I rest my forehead against his temple when I'm done.

"Better?"

"Mmhmm."

"For the record, I don't think we should stay." His jaw is set and his eyes are hard and I think I fall in love with him a little more right then.

Just until the end of the show, I promise myself. It's another twenty minutes max and then we can get out of here for some fresh air. There are two awards left, including Best Performer of the Year, which Noel is up for. I try to pay attention, I really do. I'm disappointed when the award goes to Noel's arch-nemesis Bellamy Blais instead. But I can't deny that I'm so fucking relieved when the whole thing comes to an end.

The house lights come up and Christian sets me on my feet. But before we can take even a single step, a mob descends upon us. I'm swept away by well-wishers whom I'm sure have the best of intentions. Except they're driving me farther and farther away from Christian until I can't see him over the heads of the people around me.

Keep it together, Sebastian. Smile and nod and don't lose your shit.

A hand wraps around my arm and I spin around, expecting to see Christian's beautiful face, but it's only Noel. He must've realized what was happening at the end of the show there because he does not look happy.

"Should you be here right now?" he demands.

I shake my head and try to hide behind him.

"Right. Figured."

"Christian?"

Noel cranes his neck. "Can't see him. I think he got sucked into a group of old-timers. Come on, let's get you out of here." He starts dragging me toward the side of the room.

"No, wait. Christian."

Noel glares at me. "I'll come back and tell him where you are. We need to get you out of here now."

I don't have any more fight in me. I let Noel lead me out of a side door and into an empty hallway. The noise from the party is still too loud though, so we hurry down the hall and around the corner, not stopping until the noise fades to a distant hum.

Ahead of us are stairs that descend to a set of doors and Noel carefully guides me down onto the top step, next to the handrail running down the middle. I lean against it, resting my head on the cool metal.

Noel's saying something to me, but I can't really hear him over the sound of blood rushing past my ears. There's a vise clamped around my chest. My lungs have no room to expand. My heart has forgotten how to beat.

Noel takes a step away from me and my fingers are frozen into claws around his wrist. He crouches back down next to me. "I'll be right back. Just stay still. Everything's going to be okay." He pries my hand off him and disappears.

CHAPTER
TWENTY-SIX

CHRISTIAN

God-fucking-damn it. We get mobbed so fast I completely lose sight of Sebastian and no matter how hard I try to move toward the last spot I saw him, I keep getting pushed back.

I'm surrounded by people I used to know in the industry. Executives and producers and performers from studios I've worked with in the past. If we were anywhere else, any*time* else, I would gladly chat and catch up with them. But I've got more important things to worry about than what they've done in the past ten years.

"Christian!"

Someone shoulders his way through the circle of people around me and waves his hand in my face. I flinch, then realize it's Noel.

I grab his arm. "Where's Sebastian?"

Noel doesn't answer me. He just turns and tugs me along with him. I call out an apology to no one in particular and follow Noel toward the side of the ballroom. He pushes open the door for me and points down the hall.

"He's around the corner and all the way down."

I take off. "Sebastian?" I don't see him around the corner, so I keep jogging until I spot his familiar back sitting at the top of a set of stairs. Relief floods me.

He's all hunched over, face hidden in the space he's created with his knees and arms. I rush over. "Hey."

Sebastian's shoulders rise, then sink in a shaky exhale. I sit down next to him and gently wrap my arm around his body. Sebastian curls into me, burying his face against my neck.

"Fuck, I don't know what's wrong with me."

I press a kiss to the top of his head and my chest twinges in pain for him. I wish I could take his suffering away, to somehow siphon it off so I can bear it instead. "There's nothing wrong with you."

"Then why am I like this?"

I don't have an answer to that. But all sorts of people are all sorts of ways for no reason whatsoever. That doesn't mean there's anything wrong with them. And from where I'm sitting, Sebastian is everything that is right with the world.

"I don't know, babe. But I wouldn't change a single thing about you."

Sebastian doesn't respond, just burrows deeper into me. He's starting to tremble, which is not a good sign.

"Do you need your medication? Do you have it on you?" Because I suspect the whole five things exercise will only do so much.

"It's in our hotel room."

I growl and make a mental note to remember to bring it

with us the next time we leave the house. "Okay, let's go then."

"No, wait." Sebastian clutches my lapels when I try to get up. "I can't."

I frown and do a quick scan of Sebastian's body. Did he injure himself somehow? Do I need to carry him? "Why not?"

"Because. I need to go back." He nods toward the ball-room. "Afterparties."

Anger flares up inside me—at Sebastian for pushing himself when he obviously needs to take a break, at all the people who've created an industry that makes us think we need to sacrifice ourselves to stay relevant.

"No, you don't."

"But..." Sebastian looks up at me with those big brown eyes and ridiculous lashes. "Networking and stuff."

There's so much emotion pouring off him that it feels like a tidal wave. Fear and self-recrimination, so much anxiety. I hate that he has to deal with all this. I hate that he's thinking about work and getting ahead instead of taking care of himself.

"Tell me honestly, do you really want to go and smile at all those people and pretend that everything's okay?"

Sebastian drops his chin to his chest. "Not really."

Yeah, I didn't think so. "Then we're not going."

"But..." Sebastian says again.

I cup his cheek and wrap my fingers around the back of his neck to tilt his face up. "There will always be more parties to go to, more people to network with. Opportunities will present themselves again, they always do. You don't have to be so hard on yourself. You can stop working for one night. Think of it as a reward for winning tonight."

Sebastian blinks at me and for a moment I'm sure I've lost the argument. But then he finally nods. Thank-fuck-ing-god.

"Okay. Good." I help Sebastian to his feet and guide him out of the doors in front of us. "Do you want to walk back? Or would you rather call a cab?"

"Walking's fine," Sebastian says quietly.

The night is warm and our hotel isn't far, so I tuck Sebastian under my arm and lead the way. We're silent as we walk and my mind drifts back to Sebastian up on the stage earlier. He was brilliant. His acceptance speech had been witty and gracious and I haven't been so proud of anyone in my life.

Knowing now that he was probably fighting back an anxiety attack the whole time makes me even prouder of him. He's so brave in the face of adversity, strong even when knocked down. He doesn't need me to protect him, but I want to protect him all the same.

In the elevator up to our room, Sebastian turns to wind his arms around my waist. I tuck his head under my chin and hold him until the elevator dings and the door opens on our floor. In our room, I help him out of his suit, then his shirt, then his pants until he's wearing nothing but a pair of pink boxer briefs that match the handkerchief in his breast pocket. I press Sebastian onto the bed before stripping myself down to my underwear too.

"Meds?" I ask.

Sebastian points to the bathroom. "Toiletry bag."

I grab it along with a glass of water and bring it back to the bed. "How many?" I ask, opening up the pill container.

"Just one."

I shake it out and drop it into Sebastian's hand. He swallows it down and we climb in under the covers. We find each other in the middle of the bed, heads on the same pillow, limbs tangling together.

"How are you feeling?" I ask.

"It'll take a bit for the drugs to kick in." He scoots in a little closer and his eyes flutter shut.

I press a kiss to his brow and breathe in the scent that is uniquely Sebastian. I love that smell, the way it winds itself into me and lights me up from the inside out. I'm defenseless against Sebastian's cute grins and even cuter stammering. I admire the hell out of him and what he's accomplished all on his own.

I love him.

The realization is like a flip of a switch in my mind, like a lightbulb suddenly turning on and I can finally see things clearly. From the moment he walked into Mars with those bright eyes and handed me his business card, I was a lost cause. Every single thing we've done since then, everything we've said to each other—it feels inevitable that we would end up where we are now.

No wonder I felt immediately drawn to Sebastian. No wonder I jumped at the chance to work with him. Some part of my subconscious must've recognized who he was and what he would become to me. My heart must've known that it had just met its soulmate.

I study Sebastian as he sleeps, the long fan of his eyelashes over his cheeks, the slight pout of his lips, the steady and shallow rise and fall of his breathing.

Could these feelings be the result of the camera that's constantly pointed at us? Maybe. Maybe not. I don't think I care either way. If it wasn't for the camera, I wouldn't have had the chance to spend all that time with him and learn about him and discover how wonderful he is. If it wasn't for the camera, I would never have fallen in love.

Because this protectiveness I feel for Sebastian, the compulsion I have to give him everything he needs and everything he wants—it must be love. I'll do anything to make him happy, anything to make sure he's provided for. If it means making hundreds of videos, then I'll do it. If it means diving back into the world of adult entertainment, I don't have to think twice. If it means dragging Sebastian out of its clutches, then I'll be more than willing to do that too.

He's my life now. His well-being is my well-being. His success is my success. My fate is bound up with his and that makes me so deliriously ecstatic. I grin—a full smile with teeth showing. It's silly, I know, but I can't help it. There's no way to contain this kind of joy. It's bubbling up inside me and flowing out over the top. I want to shake Sebastian awake just to tell him.

I love you. You're amazing and I love you.

I turn carefully and reach for my phone instead. I might've downloaded Instagram a while ago to better facilitate my Sebastian-stalking addiction. Now I'm glad I did it. It's awkward trying to type with one thumb without jostling Sebastian, but this isn't something I can put off. I hit the search bar and start inputting names of anyone and everyone I can think of. When the app suggests related accounts to follow, I tap on those too. It doesn't take long for people to start following me back.

CHAPTER
TWENTY-SEVEN

SEBASTIAN

I wake up to the sound of light snoring in my ear. A warm breath tickles my collarbone and a heavy arm is slung over my middle. Christian is fast asleep, curled around me like he's trying to shield me from the rest of the world.

He looks... not younger, but less guarded when he's asleep like this. His brow is relaxed and I didn't realize how much of his intense gaze came from the subtle furrow he always sports. My heart flips over in my chest and I smile at the achy fullness there.

The clock on the nightstand flashes 3:27am. Oh god. I'm groggy from crashing so hard and there's a chemical taste at the back of my tongue from my medication. I should probably get up for some water, but I don't want to leave the safety of Christian's arms.

He found me last night and brought me back here. He got me my medication and put me to bed. Like he'd been doing it for ages. Like this is a regular part of our life together.

Even when I wanted to go to the afterparties, Christian knew better. And thank god, because I can't imagine what kind of disaster that would've been. I don't know what was going through my mind that made me think I could actually survive any of those parties.

Christian taking care of me last night could be chalked up to friendship. Noel probably would've done the same if I'd asked him to. But the *way* he took care of me, the tenderness in his eyes, the gentleness of his touch, the warmth of him all wrapped up around me... it feels like more than friendship.

Maybe I'm deluding myself? Or tricking myself into seeing something that isn't there?

What would someone like Christian see in someone like me? I'm babbling most of the time, going on about nerdy stuff no one really cares about. I'm riddled with anxiety and I never know when it's going to rear its ugly head and swallow me whole.

Christian is older, he's mature, he's experienced. He's lived a whole life, then walked away from it to build a completely new one. He's so strong and steady and calm.

He doesn't need me. He could do so much better than me. And yet, here he is.

Christian stirs like maybe he heard my thoughts. He blinks blearily in the moonlight filtering in through the window.

"Hey," I whisper when he focuses on me.

"Hey." His voice is lower and more gravelly than normal and it rakes across my skin in a scintillating glide. He rubs his eyes and stretches. "Why are you awake?"

"So I can watch you sleep."

He chuckles and the vibrations travel through the

mattress to resonate in my chest. "Should I be worried about you taking advantage of me?"

I smile. "I hadn't thought of that, but now that you mention it…" I throw my leg over his hip and pull us flush to one another, chest to chest, stomach to stomach. "Maybe *you* can take advantage of *me*," I whisper against Christian's mouth.

We're both pretty gross. Neither of us have taken a shower after our sweaty jaunt down the red carpet. We're not polished and clean, primped and ready for the camera, but I haven't felt this turned on in ages. I haven't wanted Christian this badly in my life.

Our kiss is lazy and sleepy. Our hands wander in leisurely exploration. I grow hard by degrees, a slow and steady rise rather than the sudden spike of arousal that usually hits me when I'm with Christian.

He moans and his hips tilt forward, bringing our cocks together in a sizzle of heat. I whimper into Christian's mouth and he grunts in response. He kisses along my jaw, or more accurately, rubs his beard along it, then down my neck and over to my shoulder. I'm going to be covered in beard burn and I won't be able to hide it with clever collars. The thought of carrying Christian's mark publicly, of showing it off to the world—fuck, my balls tighten and my cock jumps.

"I love the way you smell," Christian mumbles against my skin before licking a path up my neck.

"What do I smell like?" Ripe is the first word that comes to mind.

"Delicious," Christian says instead. "Heavenly. Divine."

I whimper again at the verbal onslaught.

"You taste magnificent." He draws my ear between his teeth, lashing the lobe with his tongue before catching my earring. "I can't get enough of you. Fuck, I never want to let you go."

The words reach deep inside me, wind around my heart, binding me to Christian like nothing else can. "More," I beg.

He doesn't hesitate. "I love how we fit together." He arches into me as if to prove his point.

I hike my leg up a tiny bit higher to squeeze out any molecule of air that dares to try and get between us.

Christian moans in approval. "See? Perfectly matched." His hand draws down the length of my back and settles on my ass, massaging the muscles in his big hand. "Perfect fit." He dips his fingers down the back of my briefs and into my crack to find my hole. "Here too."

I shudder as he rubs slow circles around my hole. Almost zero pressure, just enough for me to know he's there.

"Remember how I fit in here?" Christian asks, tapping once.

How could I ever forget? "Yesss."

"So tight." Another tap. Feather-light.

"Yesss."

"I'd live there if I could."

"Fuck." I don't know what to do—push my hips forward to rub my dick on Christian's stomach or back to encourage his fingers into my ass. "Christian."

He hums, pressing against my hole while tightening his hold on me. "Say it again. Say my name again."

"Christian." It comes out shaky this time as my whole body vibrates under his touch.

"I fucking love how you say my name."

"Christian!"

"Sebastian." He pulls his hand away from my ass to push our underwear out of the way. "Give me your hand."

I don't need to be asked twice. I let Christian guide my hand to our cocks. Combined they're so thick I can't quite touch my thumb to my middle finger. I try anyway, squeezing tight, using our pre-cum to ease the friction as I jerk us off. Christian goes back to fingering my hole.

His cock is hard, yet velvety soft, and when it slides along mine, it sends a zing of pleasure ricocheting through me before eventually settling in my balls. The pressure builds as we rut together, as we rub ourselves over one another.

"Fuck, Sebastian. I'm so close."

"Me too. Fuck. Oh god."

We press our foreheads together, both breathing hard. Our breaths mingle, and the sweat from our bodies mix in a slippery, sopping mess.

"Sebastian," Christian grits out between clenched teeth. "Fuck, fuck!"

He kisses me, shoving his tongue into my mouth while his fingers push into my hole. The dual invasion is all I need to tip over the edge and Christian's right behind me.

We come. Hard. Thrusting against each other as we both ejaculate into my hand. It goes on and on and on until my lungs scream for air and my brain starts to short-circuit. Still, I cling to Christian, trying to wring out every last ounce of our combined orgasm.

We lay like that for a long time. Our cocks soften in my hand. Christian's fingers are still toying with my ass. We're covered in a stew of bodily fluids. I've never felt so sexy and so wanted in my entire life.

The words hover on the tip of my tongue. I want to say them so goddamn much. To whisper them against Christian's lips, so he can taste how much I mean them.

But I don't. Those three little words can flip entire worlds upside down, and the thought of losing Christian chills me to the bone. I'm not brave enough to risk it. Not today.

We fall asleep like that. Gross, but holding each other. I repeat the words over and over in my mind—*I love you. I love you. I love you*—and hope that somehow, someday, Christian will feel the same about me.

CHAPTER
TWENTY-EIGHT

CHRISTIAN

"You look happy."

I glance up from my phone to find Donnie smirking at me.

"Okay." I try to wipe the smile off my face and fail spectacularly.

"It's Sebastian, isn't it?" Donnie pulls out the other chair and sits down with me at the table in the staff break room—uninvited.

"Don't you have anything better to do?"

Donnie shakes his head. "Nope. All the spin classes are done for the day. I don't have anywhere else to be."

I go back to my phone and the brand-spanking-new Instagram account I'm trying to figure out how to use. I know it's a publicity tool and attracting as much attention as possible is the whole point of having it. But it still feels weird. I find myself constantly thinking about when and where to take pictures, and what the captions under the pictures should say. How much should I put out there? What's too much?

This must be what's going on inside Sebastian's brain all the time. Why he always has his phone in his hand, why he's always thinking about what would make a cute photo. Frankly, it's exhausting, always having to live life under a microscope of your own making. I don't know how he does it.

And then there's the type of attention I've been getting. I'm not talking about the weirdos sending me dick pics or the trolls who claim I'm going to hell. It's not even the fans who go a little berserk over every picture I post—those I recognize from back in the day.

It's the industry people, the people I used to work with. I haven't spoken to most of them in the last ten years and some I barely remember. They're all coming out of the woodwork like we've been best friends since forever. They leave comments like they know me personally. They send me messages wanting to start up conversations. The more direct ones straight up ask whether I'm free for whatever project they happen to be working on.

I'm getting serious flashbacks of those last few years where it was grind, grind, grind, smile, smile, smile, and all the while I was kind of dying inside. I can see how easy it would be to slide right back into that life like I never left it. But if I'm serious about helping Sebastian with this, about lightening his load, then I need to make sure I don't. I won't be much use to anyone if I end up drowning right next to him.

"Is that Instagram?" Donnie's leaning over to peer at my screen. "I thought you didn't do social media."

I pull my phone away. "I don't."

He cocks an eyebrow at me.

"I mean, I didn't." I lock my phone and set it face down on the table. "It's for Sebastian."

Donnie's smile grows wider.

"It's for the video," I try to deflect. "It's part of the promo and marketing stuff."

"Uh-huh."

I growl in frustration and push my chair back to go get a bottle of water from the fridge. Gavin walks in right then.

"Hey, what's going on?"

Donnie nods at me. "Christian's in love."

"Shut up. I'm not—" Except, I *am* in love. And I have more than a sneaking suspicion that Sebastian's in love with me too. That's the only way I can explain what happened in Chicago. The way he looked at me and said my name. How he clung to me while we kissed.

We woke up that last morning in each other's arms, grinning and giggling at each other like teenagers. We packed up our things and headed back to New York, holding hands and trading kisses like we're an actual couple the whole way. When I dropped him off at his apartment, we shared a goodbye kiss that's still lingering on my lips. I almost invited myself upstairs so I could spend a few more hours in his arms.

"Oh damn." Gavin takes my chair at the table and I drop onto the couch. "You really are in love, aren't you?"

I don't even need to answer. The irresistible tug of a smile on my lips gives me away.

"Is it that guy?" Gavin asks.

"Sebastian," Donnie supplies for him.

"Right, the camboy."

"And a member here," Donnie adds.

"Right!" Gavin's eyes light up at the reminder. "Shacking up with your co-star, huh?"

I glower at Gavin and his crude depiction. Sebastian and I are so far from that, that it's not remotely funny.

"So, how does that work?" Donnie asks with a genuine look of concern.

"How does what work?"

"You know, the whole sex with other people thing." Donnie and Gavin both stare at me expectantly and I honestly don't know what to tell them.

"Well, most of his stuff is solo," I say, trying to avoid the conversation they clearly want to have.

"Yeah, but he *did* have sex with other guys. Is he going to keep doing that?" Gavin asks.

I groan and slump down into the couch. We haven't even talked about whether we're a couple yet. Of course we haven't talked about sex with other performers.

Donnie leans forward and braces his elbow on his knees. "Would you be okay with it? If he did?"

How do I explain it to people who've never worked in the industry? How do I convey how unsexy shooting porn normally is?

"It's not really sex."

I get two incredulous expressions thrown back at me.

"I mean, yeah, there are dicks and mouths and holes and—" I groan and cover my face with my hands. I can't believe I'm saying this shit out loud. "It's not real. It's just physical. Like, when you're slacking while lifting weights. Sure, you might work up a sweat, and your muscles might be a little sore after, but you're not really building muscles or getting stronger because the weights are too light. You're just going through the motions."

Donnie and Gavin glance at each other like they might actually understand what I'm saying. We're all quiet for long enough that I hold out hope that we're going to move on.

Then Gavin tilts his head. "So it really wouldn't bother you?"

I know they're just trying to look out for me so I take a second to actually consider his question. Would it bother me if Sebastian kept performing with other guys? With guys like Noel, maybe, where they're friends and they get along and they care about each other.

I try to picture it. I poke at the idea. I think back to that video of Sebastian and Noel that I've jerked off to half a dozen times. I remember the awards show, meeting Noel in person, and seeing how protective he was of Sebastian. I feel something, but I don't think it's jealousy. It doesn't twist me up on the inside or make my fingers clench into fists. No, it feels more like affinity, like Noel and I have something special in common, like we're on the same side. If anything, I'm glad that Sebastian has a friend like Noel, a friend who is willing to look out for him, who came to me because he knew I was what Sebastian needed.

I look Gavin in the eye, then Donnie, more certain of my answer now than ever before. "No, it wouldn't bother me."

They exchange a look and I suspect that they don't believe me. It doesn't matter though. They don't need to believe me. I believe in Sebastian and that's enough.

My phone buzzes on the table and Gavin picks it up to check the notification.

"It's Instagram. You have new comments." He tosses the phone at me and I drop it onto the couch like it's a hot potato.

Now *there's* a problem. How do I be the Chris Preacher Sebastian needs me to be without becoming the Chris Preacher that I hate? I need to figure out where that line is before I accidentally cross it.

"You're not going to check it?" Gavin asks as he stands and stretches.

I glare at my phone and groan. "Maybe later."

Donnie's glaring at my phone too and after Gavin steps out, he comes over and gives me a clap on the shoulder. "I have to admit that I don't really understand this relationship of yours, but if it makes you happy…"

I pat his hand. "It makes me happy."

He nods solemnly and sighs. "In that case, I'm happy for you too."

CHAPTER
TWENTY-NINE

SEBASTIAN

"So… about the footage from Chicago…" I'm sitting on a barstool beside the breakfast bar in Christian's apartment.

He's standing on the opposite side, next to the stove, stirring a pot of pasta. He holds the wooden spoon in midair. "Yeah?"

"Um, I took a quick look through it…" A very quick look. Like, basically, scrolling the progress bar as fast as I could. I didn't even want to do that. In fact, there's a part of me that wants to delete the whole thing altogether.

"And?"

"And it's… well…" How can I possibly describe what little I saw? The framing was good, and the lighting looked good. Everything was in focus as far as I could tell. There was nothing wrong with the production value—it was the acting.

Or lack thereof.

The whole thing was so freaking raw. All of our feelings laid right out there for everyone to see. It's written all over both of our faces. Some people might try to call it acting, but let's be honest—we're not that good.

I've never put that much of myself out there before. Everything that gets posted for public consumption is carefully curated. It's me, but it's a very specific version of me. All the other stuff, all the ugly and inconvenient and uncomfortable stuff gets neatly hidden away. If we publish this video, it'll change all that.

Christian turns off the stove and pours the pasta through a colander. "Is there something wrong with it?"

"No, but…"

There was one thing I saw when reviewing the footage that made me ecstatic. It was the way Christian looked at me. Especially the last few minutes in the shower when we rushed at each other, smashing our mouths together. That had been entirely unscripted, completely impromptu, and it revealed so much that I actually watched it a couple times before moving on. Even now, thinking back on it, I'm getting swept away by the emotion that was so obvious between us. I know he loves me. And I want to tell him that I know.

"I love you."

Christian's in the middle of pouring a jar of tomato sauce into a small sauce pan and when his head jerks up, the tomato sauce goes flying. "Shit!"

He sets the pan on the counter, tosses the jar into the sink, and grabs the paper towels to wipe up the mess. It's on the counter, running down the cabinets and all over the floor.

"Oh crap, I'm sorry!"

"No! Don't be!" He ducks behind the kitchen cart and I scramble off the barstool to help him.

"Here, pass me some." I gesture to the paper towels and he hands me the roll. We're both crouching on the floor and it hasn't escaped my notice that he hasn't responded to my declaration. I sneak a peek at him. He's got tomato sauce on his nose.

I find a clean spot on my paper towel. "Hey, hold still." I reach for his chin and when I lift it, our gazes collide. There it is—that's what I saw. The love I feel reflected right back at me. "I love you," I say again.

Christian's chest expands in a silent gasp. "I love you." His voice breaks and before he can even get the last syllable out, I launch myself at him—tomato sauce be damned.

Christian lands on his ass with a grunt and we topple to the floor, me on top of him. I kiss his mouth, his cheeks, his eyes, his brows, his forehead, even his tomato-sauced nose. I kiss every inch of his face and pepper in those three little words in between.

"I love you. I love you. Fuck, I love you so goddamn much."

Christian's laughing. I can feel it reverberating from his chest straight into mine. He rolls us so I'm on my back and his thigh is wedged between mine. "I love you too." Then he captures my mouth in a searing kiss that I feel to the tip of my toes.

"You do?" I ask when he finally relinquishes my lips and I find the air to speak. I know he does and yet, it still so freaking surreal. Like I fell into a dream all those months ago when I walked into Mars and haven't quite woken up from it.

"I really do." There's not a single shred of doubt in Christian's voice, in the way he's staring into my eyes. "I never realized how much life I was missing out on before you waltzed into it. I never knew what it meant to care about someone so much that my every breath and every heartbeat aches for them. This thing I feel when I look at you, when I think about you—it's so big and over-whelming and sometimes it feels like I'm drowning in it, but all I want is to keep diving deeper. You're my inspira-tion. You're my bright, shining light. I don't know how I ever lived without you."

His words seep into me and fill me up with all that joy and happiness and bubbly, fuzzy goodness. I'm so full of it that it's leaking out of my eyes in tears.

"Hey." Christian wipes at the stray drops escaping down my temples. "What's wrong?"

"Nothing. I just love you so damn much."

Christian leans his forehead against mine. "I love you that much too."

We kiss again, slower this time, sweet and tender like we have all the time in the world and we're going to enjoy every second of it.

I sniffle. Something acrid teases my nostrils. "Christian?"

"Hmm?"

"Is something burning?"

"Oh shit!" He jumps to his feet and pulls the oven door open. A plume of smoke billows out and the smoke detector goes off.

We scramble. I grab the hand towel and try to fan the smoke away from the detector while Christian yanks open every window. It takes a minute for the smoke detector to calm down and by then Christian's assessed the damage.

The frozen meatballs he put into the oven are burnt to a crisp.

He turns to me and puts his hands on his hips. "Order pizza?"

I wind my arms around his waist. "Order pizza."

"I love you, Sebastian."

"I love you too, Christian."

Later, after the kitchen's cleaned up and the pizza consumed, we lie on Christian's bed together—I'm the little spoon and he's the big one. My laptop is open in front of us and I've got the footage from Chicago pulled up.

"Are you sure you want to watch this?"

Christian takes my knee and lifts it so he can wedge his thigh between my legs, right up against my taint. Then he slips his hand under my shirt and his fingers immediately latch onto a nipple. "I am," he murmurs into my ear.

I whimper as my body responds to him, as my heart swells with love for him. I hit the play button. The footage is completely unedited so there's a lot of downtime in between the good stuff and I manage to stay focused enough to jump to the exciting bits.

Like me with my foot hiked up on the bench in the shower. Christian's kneeling behind me and the camera angle perfectly captures his tongue licking my hole.

On the bed behind me, Christian hums and his fingers pinch my nipple. "Hmm, hot." His cock is growing and he shifts his hips to press it against my ass.

When we get to the messy make-out section in the shower, Christian's fingers still, his thigh stops rubbing against my crotch. "Damn," he whispers with a tone of reverence.

"Yeah."

"That's…"

"Yeah." My heart is racing—from Christian's groping or from the video or from worry about what he's going to think, I don't know. "I don't have to use this part. I mean, I wasn't planning on using this part. It wasn't in our initial plans anyway, so it's not like I really need it."

"Sebastian."

"Actually, I'm not sure about the footage at all. It's not all like this, but it's still a lot. I totally understand if you don't want to show it to the entire world. Honestly, I'm not sure how I feel about it myself."

"Sebastian." Christian slips his hand under my waist and tugs and suddenly I'm on my back and he's pinning me to the bed.

"Huh?"

"Breathe."

I suck in a breath and oh right, I wasn't breathing.

"You okay?"

I feel Christian's delicious, heavy weight on me. I smell the lingering scent of tomato sauce in the air. I see the love shining in Christian's eyes. My heart settles down and my mind stops whirring. "Yeah, I'm okay."

"What would you like to do with this footage?"

I sigh. "I don't know."

Christian nods then plants a kiss on the corner of my mouth. "If you want to use it, I'm cool with that. If you want to reshoot, I'm cool with that too. I trust your judgment."

"You'd be willing to reshoot?"

"Of course."

I frame Christian's handsome face with my hands. "Why in the world would you love me?"

He chuckles and shakes his head like the answer is obvious. "Because you're brilliant."

My chest expands with love until I'm sure I'm going to explode.

"You're brilliant, Sebastian, and I love you."

CHAPTER
THIRTY

SEBASTIAN

I have to edit this damn thing but it is literally the absolute last thing I want to do. I'm just... not sure how to do it, how to cut it all together so it's not too much. I've sat myself down in front of my computer and watched the footage a dozen times already. I've tried to pretend that it's two strangers on the screen so I wouldn't feel too close to it. I've taken breaks, gone for runs to clear my mind, and every time I open up the window again, I hurdle straight into a mental wall.

It's just so raw. The way we look at each other, the way we touch each other. I called Christian by his full name several times because that's who I was having sex with—Christian, not Chris Preacher. There are no cum shots, not even a cream pie. I don't think anyone could argue that our orgasms were fake, but fans like seeing the cum. That's what they pay the big bucks for.

I've toyed with the idea of recording an apology to explain why the video ends the way it has to—without the cum shot. But it feels kind of ridiculous and why the hell should I need to apologize anyway? Christian and I had really hot, really intimate sex. We filmed it and we're letting the whole world watch it. Shouldn't that be enough?

I set my laptop off to the side and flop down on my bed.

Fans are still rabid over #Chastian online. Our public appearances in Chicago have only fueled the frenzy, which ironically, is what we wanted to do. Only now we have to deliver on all the teasers we've put out there. And fast. Attention spans are short these days. If we don't produce content, fans will get bored and move on.

My phone buzzes and I roll over to check it.

NOEL

Have you seen this?

It's a link to an Instagram account profile.

Chris Preacher. "Legendary" adult performer. One half of #Chastian.

I sit up and stare at my phone. What the hell? Christian doesn't have an Instagram account. He doesn't have any social media. I would know.

There are a few photos posted already. Ones of us from Chicago and from some of our "dates." Other selfies he's taken in bathroom mirrors. Those look like they were taken at Mars. He's shirtless and if he's wearing pants, they're riding too low for the camera to capture.

He's up to a thousand followers already and he couldn't have created the account that long ago. Maybe while we were in Chicago? In the few days since we've gotten back?

The link on his profile goes to *my* OnlyFans page and I'm stunned. I honestly don't know how I'm supposed to feel about this. Happy that Christian's jumping on the promo bandwagon? Grateful? Guilty that he feels he needs to be more active on social media for my sake?

Yes, that's the one—guilty. It creeps through me, slithery and slimy and gross. He didn't need to do this. I hate that I might have pressured him into something I know he doesn't want to do.

I check the time. Christian's still at work for several more hours, but if I'm lucky, maybe I can catch him between appointments. I stuff my phone in my pocket and head for the door.

Christian is finishing up with a client when I get to Mars so I grab a seat by the juice bar and shoot Noel a text to.

SEBASTIAN

How did you find this?

NOEL

It's everywhere. Everyone's talking about it. How did you not know?

I don't know. I've been busy.

More like distracted.

I send him a middle finger emoji.

I look up from my phone to see Christian coming toward me. His eyes are locked on mine, his lips are curled into a smile that makes me think he's going to devour me.

I stand to greet him and he pulls me right into a kiss like I haven't seen him in weeks—it's only been hours.

"Hey," he whispers against my lips.

"Hey."

"This is a nice surprise."

I snort and hold up my phone. "You're one to talk about surprises."

Christian's brow furrows, then shoots up to his hairline. He reaches up to rub the back of his neck. "Oh. That," he says with a hesitant expression.

"Yeah. That."

He sighs and drops into the chair I vacated, then pulls me into his lap. I loop my arm around his neck as he settles me snugly against him.

"Not that I'm complaining or anything, but... why did you do it?"

He shrugs. "You work so hard and I wanted to do something to help. It seemed like the easiest and fastest thing to get going. Is that okay?"

I chuckle and tilt my head. "You're asking me? I should be asking you."

Christian plants a kiss on the corner of my lips and sighs. "Honestly?"

I scowl. "Of course, honestly."

He winces. "I'm not sure yet."

Fuck. That guilt wriggles up in me and makes my stomach turn. "You really don't have to. Especially since you retired because of burnout. Social media is worse than anything you had back then."

Christian puts his hand on my chest, on top of my heart. "Maybe. But if there's a chance that it'll make life easier for you, then I want to try."

The guilt stops squirming, smothered by the love Christian's pouring into me. I mimic his position, putting my hand over his heart. "Thank you."

I kiss him, slow and sweet, nothing rushed or frantic. Like the earth is standing still, giving us all the time we need.

"You're going to have to teach me about social media," Christian says against my lips. "I don't know how you keep up with it all the time."

I snort. "We'll set some ground rules. I don't want you relapsing because of me."

"And I don't want you working yourself into anxiety attacks."

I roll my eyes because Christian's got a point. "Fine. Neither of us will work too hard. How's that?"

"That's good."

"And we might want to consider upgrading your phone."

"What's wrong with my phone?"

"It could use a better camera."

Christian huffs. "Does this mean we're officially number sign Chastian?"

I pull back far enough to frown at him. "Hashtag."

Christian's lips quirk into a smile.

"But you knew that."

"I have to live up to the old geezer image, don't I?"

"Jesus, what have I created?"

"You love me."

I gaze into Christian's eyes and feel that love well up inside me. It fills every nook and cranny, every dark corner, and every forgotten recess. "I do."

"Christian!"

We both turn toward the front desk where Sawyer's waving him over.

"Shit. I've got to go. My next client's probably here."

I reluctantly slide off his lap, but I can't bring myself to pull my hands from him. They linger on his chest, his stomach, his waist. "Come over after you finish work?"

Christian bends to plant a quick kiss on my lips. "I'll pick up dinner on the way."

He takes my hand and holds on to it as he walks backward away from me. We don't let go until both our arms are outstretched with only our fingertips touching. When he disappears around the corner, I catch Sawyer rolling his eyes and shaking his head.

"Jesus, the two of you," he says with a smile. "I'll get a cavity just watching you."

I smile back at him. "Then don't watch!" Because I have no plans of dialing down the lovey-dovey with Christian. I only want to dial it up.

I float all the way back to my apartment and when I pull my computer into my lap, it's like some kind of switch has flipped inside me. I can edit this damn thing all of a sudden. Maybe it's knowing that Christian is all-in on this venture with me, that we're doing this together, as a team. I'm seeing all that raw emotion in a different light now. Instead of making me uncomfortable, I find that I can't tear my eyes away. I linger on the way Christian's fingers press into my skin, that bead of sweat rolling down his neck. The sound of my gasp tugs at something base and elemental in my gut. This is two people, loving each other, pouring themselves out for one another, leaving nothing in reserve. It's beautiful. It's powerful. It's by far the best thing I've ever produced.

I work straight through the afternoon, my fingers flying as I edit. I barely have to think. My brain has taken on a life of its own, operating in some kind of weird trance that completely bypasses any conscious decision-making. I'm deep into it when the buzzer sounds on my door, snapping me back into reality.

It's dark outside. The only light in my apartment comes from the screen of my laptop. My stomach is grumbling about being ignored for too long. I grab my phone and find a few messages from Christian.

CHRISTIAN

Done work. Heading out. Want anything for dinner?

I'm going to pick up Chinese.

You better not still be working.

Shit. I run to the intercom and press the button to let Christian into the building. Then I open my door and listen for his footsteps as he climbs up the stairs.

"Sorry," I say when his head pops up over the steps. "I lost track of time."

He pins me with a scolding look. "I figured." He draws me into his arms and gives me a hello kiss that makes me want to abandon dinner altogether and drag him straight to bed.

Christian smells a little sweaty from the gym. His beard rasps against my lips. His hands burn through my clothes. My dick was semi-hard from editing the video and now it's poking Christian in the thigh. He laughs, the rumble reverberating through me.

"Someone's horny."

"You're hot."

"Hmm." He walks me backward into the apartment, then pauses. "Why is it so dark in here?"

"Oh." I reach for the light switch. "I forgot to turn the light on."

Christian sighs as he places the bag of takeout on the little table in my kitchen. "You have to stop working so hard."

"I didn't mean to!" I protest. "I was on a roll!"

"What were you working on?" He asks, pulling out containers of food that make my mouth salivate.

"Our video."

Christian glances up at me, a question in his eyes. "How's that going?"

"Good!" I turn and grab my laptop. "Want to see? It's still super rough, but oh my god, it's going to be so freaking amazing."

Christian takes the laptop from me and puts it back onto the bed. "I'd love to see it. Maybe after we've eaten."

I offer him a sheepish smile and take the pair of disposable wooden chopsticks he hands me.

"So you've decided to go ahead with using the footage?" Christian asks. He's sitting in my armchair and I'm perched on the edge of my bed. He's got a container of General Tao's chicken and I've got one of beef and broccoli.

I nod. "Is that okay with you?" He's said before that he was cool with whatever I decided, but I'm not going to release anything until he gives me the okay.

He looks me straight in the eyes. "I trust you."

My breath catches in my chest. That bowls me over harder than any declaration of love. This is deeper, more intimate, more honest. Christian sees me, he knows me, and he's willing to follow my lead. It's humbling.

Christian sets his box of food aside and then takes mine from me as well. We sit on the bed, facing each other, my hands in his. "Whatever you think is best—for the business or for us—I'm game."

He says that and yet, I feel like I need to give him at least one more out. A no questions asked, no-hurt-feelings way to step away from this world that I've dragged him back into. I know first-hand how demanding it is to exist in the public eye, to hustle every single day, to have people want more and more from me. Christian's been burned before, and the last thing I want is to put him in that position again.

"You're supposed to be retired," I say. "You only agreed to do one video."

Christian's brow furrows and his eyes narrow like he knows what I'm doing and he doesn't approve. "Sebastian, you've never forced me into anything I wasn't willing to do. I mean, you're persuasive, but you're not that persuasive."

That pulls a quiet chuckle out of me. Christian says he trusts me, so I guess I need to trust him too. Trust that he knows what he's doing and what he's getting himself into. That he wants to be here, with me, and that he'll tell me if anything changes.

"In that case…" I reach for my phone. "Selfie?"

Christian rolls his eyes but pulls me down onto the bed so we're all snuggled together. I snap a few of us both looking at the camera. Then some with Christian nuzzling my cheek. Then of us kissing.

Later, after we've both posted to our social media

accounts, I scroll back through the pictures from the past several months. It tells a story. Our story.

I have nothing to worry about with the video, I realize. It's not going to show the world anything that isn't already out there. We love each other. So much so that we couldn't hide it even if we wanted to. And I don't want to. Not now. Not ever.

EPILOGUE

CHRISTIAN

Sebastian is sitting between my legs on the couch and my chin is hooked over his shoulder. His phone is propped up in some contraption, the camera pointed at us and we're live-streaming something called an Ask Me Anything. Apparently, the fans tune in, they're allowed to ask us anything, and we're supposed to answer them.

I wasn't sure how I felt about this when Sebastian first brought it up, but he said we'd skip over anything we didn't want to talk about. Besides, Sebastian's running the show. I'm just the pretty background.

The little number at the bottom of the screen that shows how many people are watching us is frighteningly high. I had no idea these things drew in so many people. I should have guessed, though, considering how well #Chastian, the Sequel is doing right now, but it's still jarring to watch that number tick up into the thousands.

Sebastian is going on about his favorite ice cream

flavor. He likes gelato better than ice cream, and then it's a toss-up between strawberry and lemon. But he hates mint, because why would he want to eat toothpaste?

He turns to me. "How about you, babe?"

My favorite ice cream flavor? I've never given it much thought before. "Vanilla. Because that's what you smell like."

His expression goes soft and he ducks his chin in a shy and sultry smile. The same one that first ensnared me. Then he puts a hand on my cheek and kisses me—opened mouth, lots of tongue. On his phone, the screen explodes in heart and fire reactions and comments about how cute we are.

They're not wrong. We're pretty damn cute. Even I can admit that.

"Okay, we've got time for one more question!" Sebastian leans forward to read the comments flying across the screen. There was one about what kind of underwear we wear and whether we're selling dirty pairs as merch—Sebastian's ignored that one, thank god. There were a few asking for fitness and nutrition tips. I deflected with something about finding a local personal trainer who can give individualized advice. The most frequently asked question is when we're going to film another video.

Sebastian sits back and nestles himself against my chest. "What do you think, babe? Another video? Don't you think two are enough?"

We knew this question was coming and Sebastian was savvy enough to draw up a little script for us to tease them with. "We wouldn't want to disappoint the fans," I say.

"Yeah, but we just put the last one out. Don't you think they want to see something else?"

Various forms of "NOOO!!!" flood the comments.

Sebastian giggles and that wonderful bubbly feeling races up my spine. I love it when he does that. I want to hear him laugh every single day for the rest of my life.

We end the Ask Me Anything and we let ourselves topple over on the couch. Sebastian flips himself over so he's straddling my hips. I've been chubby for the last hour with him squirming between my legs, but now that he's grinding his ass on my dick, it's coming fully to life.

I groan as Sebastian kisses me. Our tongues slide together and I shudder with want. I always want him. A look, a smile, a gentle caress is all it ever takes for me to be ready. He's my everything. He's all I need.

Sebastian sighs into our kiss, then lays his head down on my shoulder. I wrap my arms around him, soaking in the weight of his body on mine, his angles and planes that fit so perfectly with mine.

This is it. This is the life for me. No matter what happens in the future, whether Sebastian sticks with camming or decides to do something else, I'm in this, with him, forever.

"Move in with me," I blurt out, surprising even myself. It's only been two months since we came back from Chicago, since we admitted our love to each other, but it feels like the right thing to do, the right time to do it.

Sebastian props his chin on my chest. "Really?" His brows are raised and there's a little crease in between them.

I think fast. "Yeah, we don't have to stay here. We can get a bigger place with two bedrooms so you can use one as your studio."

It makes sense. He spends most nights at my place

already, so there's no point in paying rent for two places. Plus, with the extra income our videos are bringing in, we can afford something nicer.

I can see all these considerations running through Sebastian's mind already. "It's not a bad idea." His smile turns sheepish. "Remember that idea I had about starting my own production company?"

"Yeah." My heart leaps in my chest.

"Maybe the studio could double as my office. You know, with a desk and chair and stuff if I'm going to be working behind the scenes on more projects?" Sebastian's been dreaming of ways to expand his business, to take things to the next level. He wants to do more directing and producing on larger scale videos, almost like his own independent studio.

I can imagine him doing that already. My boyfriend, a hot-shot adult entertainment director-producer. "I think that's a great idea."

"Yeah." He gets a twinkle in his eye and pushes off my chest. "We can start looking now."

I chuckle as he grabs his phone to dive into research. He doesn't get very far before he groans, glaring at his phone.

"What's wrong?"

"Noel. He's getting all worked up about Bellamy Blais."

I'm not entirely clear what that whole thing is about. All I know is their mutual hatred of each other is the hottest gossip floating around the porn world. "What's going on now?"

"Who the hell knows? Bellamy posted something

vague online and Noel's convinced it's a dig at him. Now he's trying to plot revenge." Sebastian's brows grow more furrowed by the second.

This is not what I want the rest of our evening to be. I take the phone out of his hand, ignoring his sputtering protests. "Not now. I've got other plans for us tonight."

I pull Sebastian to his feet and then into the bedroom.

"Oh yeah? Like what?"

"Like this." I catch his lips and lick into his mouth. I slide my hands under the waistband of his sweats and palm his ass.

Sebastian whimpers and winds his arms around my neck to melt against me. I pull his cheeks apart and inch my fingers toward his hole. I freeze when they brush against something that shouldn't be there.

Sebastian grins against my mouth. "Surprise?"

I push on the butt plug and Sebastian's eyes roll toward the back of his head as he shudders. I grip the base and give it a twist. Sebastian lets out a soft, desperate sound.

"When did you put this in?" I growl.

Sebastian's not answering me anytime soon. He's writhing, grinding his erection into mine while trying to push his ass more firmly against my hand. I shove my tongue into his mouth and fuck him from both directions.

His cries are muffled by our kiss. His fingers dig into my shoulders, the back of my neck. I can tell he's close to coming when he finds the strength to pull away.

"Wait, wait. Not yet. I want you inside me."

I growl again and we start ripping our clothes off each other. We tumble onto the bed and when I slide into him, my soul melds with his. This is home. Me and Sebastian. In my apartment or his, or in someplace entirely new. Wherever Sebastian is, that's where I belong.

———

BONUS SCENE

I take the stairs two at a time. "Sebastian?"

It's quiet upstairs, but when I peer into the guest bedroom, Sebastian is exactly where I expected to find him. On the bed, laptop open, headphones on. He's hunched over, brow furrowed, staring at the screen with intense concentration.

He's working. I should've known. For some reason, I'd assumed that moving behind the camera with his new production company would mean a better work-life balance for Sebastian. I don't know what I was thinking. Of course Sebastian would work harder now than he ever has before. The upside is that The Camboy Network is taking off faster than either of us had anticipated. The downside is Sebastian has forgotten how to take a break.

"Sebastian."

He jumps in surprise, then pulls his headphones down around his neck with a sheepish grin. "Oh, hey."

To read the rest of the bonus scene, sign up for Linden Bell's Very Important Reader newsletter here: bit.ly/sebas tianbonus.

———

BELLAMY

Do you like enemies to lovers, grumpy/sunshine, opposites attract romances? Watch Noel and Bellamy face off in the next The Camboy Network book, *Bellamy*, bit.ly/bellamybm.

THANK YOU

If you've enjoyed *Sebastian*, please consider recommending it to your friends. Leave a review on social media, your own blog, Amazon, or Goodreads so other MM romance lovers can get to know Sebastian and Christian too.

If you would like to stay up to date on future Linden Bell books, join the Very Important Reader mailing list here: bit.ly/VIRSebastian.

You can also follow me on:
    Facebook - facebook.com/authorlindenbell
    Instagram - instagram.com/authorlindenbell
    Amazon - amazon.com/author/lindenbell
    Goodreads - goodreads.com/authorlindenbell
    Bookbub - bookbub.com/authors/linden-bell

ABOUT LINDEN BELL

Linden Bell writes romances that heat you up and make you smile. She's a lifelong fan of the happily ever after, and has recently admitted to being a Trekkie.

- facebook.com/authorlindenbell
- instagram.com/authorlindenbell
- amazon.com/author/lindenbell
- goodreads.com/authorlindenbell
- bookbub.com/authors/linden-bell

ALSO BY LINDEN BELL

Mars Fitness Series

Where the jocks of Mars Fitness meet the nerds of their dreams.

The Camboy Network Series

When sex on camera turns into love behind the scenes.

www.ingramcontent.com/pod-product-compliance
Lightning Source LLC
Chambersburg PA
CBHW030810210726
48290CB00002B/524